©Nao Watanuki

Toshio Sa
Illustration b
Nao Watan

D0611822

Suppose

a Kid from the LAST DUNGEON
BOONIES Moved to a Starter Town

Riho Flavin
A skilled mercenary. Approaches Lloyd in hopes of making him her cash cow.

Lloyd Belladonna
A boy from a legendary town. The weakest in his village but the strongest person in the royal capital.

©Nao Watanuki

Marie the Witch
The proprietor of Lloyd's lodgings. But what is her true identity...?

He's the
one who
lifted the
curse...

©Nao Watanuki

It was him...

Selen Hemein

A girl from a noble family. Bound by an irremovable cursed belt for years, but her fate begins to change after meeting Lloyd...!

[CONTENTS]

©Nao Watanuki

Suppose a Kid from the Last Dungeon Boonies Moved to a Starter Town

1

Toshio Satou

Illustration by
Nao Watanuki

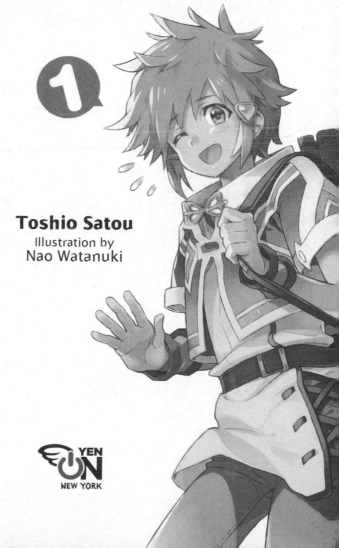

YEN ON
NEW YORK

Suppose a Kid from the LAST DUNGEON BOONIES moved to a Starter Town ❶

TOSHIO SATOU

Translation by Andrew Cunningham
Cover art by Nao Watanuki

TATOEBA LAST DUNGEON MAENO MURANO SHOUNEN GA JYOBAN NO MACHI DE
KURASUYOUNA MONOGATARI volume 1
Copyright © 2017 Toshio Satou
Illustrations copyright © 2017 Nao Watanuki
All rights reserved.
Original Japanese edition published in 2017 by SB Creative Corp.

This English edition is published by arrangement with SB Creative Corp., Tokyo in care of Tuttle-Mori Agency, Inc., Tokyo.

English translation © 2019 by Yen Press, LLC

Yen On
150 West 30th Street, 19th Floor
New York, NY 10001

Visit us at yenpress.com · facebook.com/yenpress · twitter.com/yenpress · yenpress.tumblr.com · instagram.com/yenpress

First Yen On Edition: November 2019

Yen On is an imprint of Yen Press, LLC.
The Yen On name and logo are trademarks of Yen Press, LLC.

The publisher is not responsible for websites (or their content) that are not owned by the publisher.

Library of Congress Cataloging-in-Publication Data
Names: Satou, Toshio, author. | Watanuki, Nao, illustrator. | Cunningham, Andrew, 1979– translator.
Title: Suppose a kid from the last dungeon boonies moved to a starter town / Toshio Satou ; illustration by Nao Watanuki ; translation by Andrew Cunningham.
Other titles: Tatoeba last dungeon maeno murano shounen ga jyoban no machi de kurasuyouna. English
Description: First Yen On edition. | New York, NY : Yen ON, 2019–
Identifiers: LCCN 2019030186 | ISBN 9781975305666 (v. 1 ; trade paperback)
Subjects: CYAC: Adventure and adventurers—Fiction. | Self-esteem—Fiction.
Classification: LCC PZ7.1.S266 Tat 2019 | DDC [Fic]—dc23
LC record available at https://lccn.loc.gov/2019030186

ISBNs: 978-1-9753-0566-6 (paperback)
          978-1-9753-0567-3 (ebook)

10 9 8 7 6 5 4 3 2 1

LSC-C

Printed in the United States of America

Lloyd Belladonna

An excessively strong villager from the town of legend. Earnest, kind, and honest. A people pleaser who knows little of the real world—or his own strength. Travels to the royal capital with dreams of becoming a soldier.

Selen Hemein

The Cursed Belt Princess. Freed from her long-held curse upon meeting Lloyd.

Marie the Witch

A beautiful information merchant from the royal capital. Hosts Lloyd at her house for...reasons.

Alka

The chief of the legendary town. Dotes on Lloyd like her own son.

Merthophan Dextro

A colonel and instructor at the military academy. Always on the prowl for young talent.

Allan Lidocaine

A heavily decorated young fighter. Expected to do great things at the military academy.

Riho Flavin

A skilled mercenary. In it for the money. Planning on riding Lloyd's coattails when he makes it big.

Chrome Molybdenum

The cafeteria owner who hires Lloyd. But what is his real identity...?

Choline Sterase

A female instructor at the military academy. First to realize Lloyd's true potential.

Prologue

Everyone in town loved to tell Lloyd Belladonna the same thing.

"It's too much for you."

He was a good-looking boy with a gentle smile who was much better at cooking, cleaning, and laundry than he was at throwing hands, just as his meek demeanor suggested. Even he agreed with the general consensus that he was the weakest man in town. Not a day went by without at least one village girl commenting on how he'd make a great wife someday.

No matter how many times he dived into the river, he'd never come up with a single fish. If he went to fetch firewood, it would take him until sundown to gather less than the average man. If he engaged in some friendly sparring with the other men, he'd spend the entirety of the following day in bed—and on and on and on.

So when he'd suddenly announced that he was leaving town to be a soldier in the royal capital...well, given his earnest, friendly, and gullible disposition, most people felt he should never be allowed to leave the village, let alone join the army.

Yet where Lloyd usually gave in to peer pressure, he stood his ground this time. A whiff of actual determination emerged from beneath that naive exterior. Biting his lip, he'd insisted this was what he wanted.

This new side of him flummoxed the villagers. When they'd reached their wit's end trying to convince him, they held an intervention, hoping the village chief would be able to talk some sense into him.

Ordinarily, the only things that brought this many villagers together were event planning, discussions on new laws, and more event planning. This proved just how much everyone cared about Lloyd's well-being.

A few days after he'd first started talking about enlisting in the army, the village leaders finished work in the early afternoon and dragged him to the chief's house.

On a windswept plateau with a view of the wheat fields north of the village, Lloyd sat cowering like a scolded puppy. On his side was the person who'd raised him and who Lloyd called Grandpa. Around them, the village leaders sat in silence, their faces betraying their worries and frustrations.

The stress had Lloyd sweating bullets. The spring breeze brushed across his face, carrying the scent of the green wheat stalks, and made a linen curtain sway. A sweet voice came from behind it.

"Sorry for makin' y'all wait."

A girl emerged wearing a silk robe, her black hair in twin pigtails. She looked to be around twelve years old. She was the village chief, Alka.

She might be itty-bitty, but don't let appearances fool you. She was well over a hundred—nobody knew exactly how old she was, herself included. According to her, she "became immortal to save the world, blah blah blah." But not a single villager believed this, and the entire concept had become a running joke. Basically, she was your typical *loli* grandma…but if she heard you say that, you'd end up buried neck-deep in the field for three days and nights.

Regardless of her actual age, Chief Alka spoke and acted like a middle schooler. Clutching the excess length of her robe off the ground, she pattered over to the seat of honor and plopped herself down into a legless chair made of woven bamboo. It creaked as she sat, breaking the silence.

After a brief pause, she spoke to Lloyd as if she was catching up with her grandson.

"Lloyd…I hear ya want to be a soldier in the capital, eh?"

Before he could reply, his guardian erupted, "Please talk him out of it! It's too much for him! He's always had a stubborn streak, and it shows up at the worst times!"

Lloyd wasn't about to let that pass. "We won't know…if it's too much for me…if I don't even try…"

"Do you even hear yourself?! You're a fool! You can barely gather firewood; you've never caught a fish… The army would never take you!"

"S-sure, I've never succeeded in catching a fish. But I'm sure they have other food in the capital. I'll be fine… And yeah, I'm not great at diving, but…how often will I need to dive in the city anyway?"

His rebuttal was answered by a plump older lady, who scolded him like he was her own son. "Lloyd! That's not what your grandpa means. He's worried about how feeble you are!"

His grandfather nodded vigorously, grunting. "Indeed."

"Darn tootin'. I reckon ya can't be a soldier if you can't do even these simple tasks. And there's a limit to how no-account you can be."

"Seriously, dude. Stop looking for loopholes." Next up to berate Lloyd was a stoic young man with an old sword at his hip. "You gotta admit you're the only one to blame for not rising to the occasion and overcoming your failures."

"Urp." Lloyd hung his head.

But the young man was relentless and scowled as he spitefully added, "I mean, to begin with, how can you do anything if you can barely stay underwater for an hour?"

"That's right, three hours is the clear minimum. When your grandfather was younger, he could stay under for three days!"

"Four!" his guardian boasted, holding up four fingers.

(Side note: Professional pearl divers can stay under for an average of five minutes without equipment, and the world record is just over twenty-two. FYI.)

Lloyd's grandfather spent a few moments basking in the praise of the other villagers, but he soon resumed his stern expression and glared at Lloyd once more.

"Listen up, Lloyd. Ya can't be struggling to kill a fish just because it's got a few fangs and some horns. I'm sure they've got more gnarly ones in the ocean!"

"But in novels, they talk about fish in the capital having no fangs or horns, and they apparently eat those!"

"Don't talk nonsense! How's a fish supposed to survive without 'em? If anything like that existed, I reckon they'd have been all caught immediately and gone extinct years ago."

"Erk, good point…"

(Side note: The organisms they're calling "fish" are actually monsters called "killer piranha." Sturdy horns, giant mouths, and a row of teeth capable of consuming a whole cow in three big chomps—even a hardened warrior would be helpless against them underwater.)

Spying Lloyd's resolve flagging, a woodcutter dressed in work clothes joined the pile-on.

"Even if you aren't much of a swimmer, I think you oughtta be a bit better at cutting or gathering wood…" He spoke softly, patiently, trying to get through to him.

Lloyd's grandfather mimed an ax swing. "Yes! You've gotta sneak up on the treants and take 'em down with a single blow!"

Lloyd leaned forward with an objection of his own. "But, Grandpa, in books and novels, they say they don't have to use treants in the capital, just normal beeches and cedars!"

"*Sigh*… You believe everything you read in books?" His grandfather shook his head, wiping the sweat from his brow.

"Lloyd," the woodcutter interjected, frowning. He couldn't let this slide. "If you use a normal tree for firewood, it would only last for three hours, tops. Treants burn for three whole days! You see the difference, right?"

"Yup. Even an idiot knows which is better! You'd never make it through the winter burning them piddly or'nary trees."

"I know treants are better, but…"

(Side note: Treants are terrifying monsters in the shapes of trees that stab passersby with their roots, sucking nutrition out of them. Normally, these treacherous trees vanish when they're cut down, but if you fell them before they notice you or if you get very lucky, they leave wood behind that is extremely valuable and sells for a high price. It wasn't normally used for firewood. If any merchants saw someone burning treant wood, they'd let out a bloodcurdling shriek for sure.)

The woodcutter leaned back against a pillar, folding his arms, speaking at length about his trade. "Woodcutting is a hard profession. This town has homes and warm places to stay in winter thanks to the sweat of our brows. Whether it be firewood or fish, you can't just dismiss it by saying you'll buy it! That attitude alone makes you unfit to be a soldier."

That hit Lloyd hard.

When he saw that, the woodcutter hastily added, "Er, that is…I'm not saying you have to learn all the tricks of my trade before you can go to the capital. Walking without making a sound, blending perfectly into the forest—these might not be skills you need in the city."

(Sorry to burst your bubble, but woodcutters shouldn't need those skills, either.)

"…I apologize. I got a little worked up," he continued.

Lloyd kept his head down, starting to regret his rash decision to announce that he wanted to enlist.

The young man with the sword spoke up again, his tone pointed. "The problem isn't what kind of fish they have, dude. The biggest problem is that you're trying to become a soldier even though you're super weak."

"I know you're much stronger than I am."

"When we were sparring together the other day, I held back a lot, you know. But you were still in bed for a full day afterward! …Everyone thought *I* was the bad guy, like I'd been bullying you or some shit."

"Urp…"

The young man shook his head. "*Sigh*… Plus, you should be able to heal a broken bone in an hour, max."

"It wasn't just one! I had compound fractures all over the place! That's why it took a full day!"

"Listen to yourself! Everything should heal in three hours, and I'm being liberal here! Your grandpa used to heal them with one long scream!"

(Side note: A broken bone is usually considered a serious injury, and it'll leave you stuck in a cast for at least a month...although I think you know that already.)

The young man drew his old-timey sword with a hilt decorated with two snakes, brandishing it as he lectured. "For one thing! A blow from this old thing shouldn't be breaking bones! What was this dull lump's name again? Girlsbar?"

"Something like that. Currybar? Excalibur? No, maybe Klondikebur?"

(Side note: This ancient blade's name is definitely Excalibur, the mystic sword that the legendary King Arthur used to cut down 960 enemies. It's a pretty famous sword that went by other names—including Caliburn or Callibrand.)

"That's right, Klondikebur. Yum. Sounds like a frozen treat."

The mystic blade was not getting much respect. No one even noticed that the real name had come and gone with the wind.

"I swear, if my dad hadn't foisted this thing on me, I sure wouldn't stoop to using anything this dull... Anyway, if you get hurt from crap like this, you'll never get anywhere."

Jumping off of this point, his grandfather tried a new angle. "And, Lloyd, it isn't only yer physical strength. Your magic is useless as tits on a bull!"

"Oh, right... Can you cast *anything?*"

Lloyd had winced the moment this topic was mentioned.

"Uh," he started, reluctantly. "I know the procedural stuff, but...the only spell that really works is that one that makes it rain..."

The young man shook his head dramatically. "Geez, rain falls on its own even if you don't do anything! You oughtta at least be able to make boulders fall from the sky like the chief... What were those called? Meteors?"

"Darn right," the chief purred. "Oh, shucks. That sure takes me back! I remember using 'em to drive off those monsters that appeared in the mountains 'round back."

"Those things were really something. They kept going on about how they were gonna 'destroy the world' because there were 'too many humans.' Ha-ha-ha!"

Hmm, it seemed this started a stream of reminiscing.

"And get a load of this! The other day, one showed up in human form, yapping on and on 'bout something. When we had it backed into a corner, it was all, 'It's been a long time since I assumed this form!' and turned into some sort of lizard thing! I laughed my ass off!"

"Why not show up that way in the first place? You took it down while we were fetching the chief, right?" someone asked the older lady.

"Yeah, I just gave it a few whacks with my broom, and that was all she wrote. But it took forever to clean up and—!"

They veered so far off topic that the general vibe was starting to resemble a banquet, so Alka clapped her hands a couple of times to get everyone back on track.

There was a moment of uncomfortable silence.

"That's enough of that," Alka said. "Lloyd."

"Y-yes?"

"Ya heard everyone out. But I reckon you're not changin' your mind, right?"

"Right."

She took a long look at the quiet passion in his eyes.

The time has finally come, she thought. *I was hopin' making him read all them books about soldiers would get his imagination going.*

That certainly sounds like an ulterior motive. She gave Lloyd a kind smile that betrayed none of the satisfaction of seeing her plans pay off.

"All righty. I'll let ya leave this village and become one of them soldiers in the royal capital."

""Chief!"" the entire crowd yelled as they leaped up to their feet.

"Quiet down," Alka ordered, raising a hand. "I reckon ya experience true growth by gettin' out of your bubble. Lloyd needs to widen his horizons."

©Nao Wata

"But, Chief…!"

"And once a man makes his mind up, who are we to argue?" With that, Alka turned back to Lloyd, like a mother looking at her child. "But if it gets too hard, you come right on back, you hear? …This is your home."

"Th-thanks!"

Everyone who saw her face knew the chief was taking this harder than anyone.

Meanwhile, Alka herself was thinking… *I reckon it'll be hard to not see Lloyd every day, but…I can secretly teleport over. Darn right. And the other villagers ain't gonna be there to interfere when I flirt with him!*

…If the other villagers had known what was running through her head, they'd have been left speechless for a very different reason.

And thus, Lloyd was permitted to leave for the big city.

Once Lloyd's departure was set in stone, the days flew by, each moment a bittersweet reminder of how much he loved the village and how much the villagers loved him.

And finally, the big day arrived. The sky was an unbroken sea of blue, as if celebrating the start of his new journey. Beneath the sun stood Lloyd, wearing sturdy canvas pants and a lightweight linen shirt, a small knapsack slung over his shoulder—the sort of outfit that would make you go, "Wait, are you taking a day trip?"

He had on an apologetic expression.

This was largely because the entire village had put off their work to come see him off. The beautiful carved wooden (treant) arch over the town gate was surrounded by villagers.

At the center of the crowd was Alka. She took a step forward, looking Lloyd right in the eye. "I'd love to escort ya part of the way, but…this is where the learning process begins. Ya gotta go by yourself."

In truth, the villagers had expressed their worries that she'd never come back if she went with him now. The entire town was of the opinion that the *loli* hag's doting knew no bounds. Lloyd alone was oblivious to this—he simply nodded, looking sad as he said yes.

Then his guardian stepped forward and slapped him on the back. "The royal capital's at the southernmost end of the continent! I reckon it'll only take two days if you make a run for it! Consider it good training!"

"Ah-ha-ha, that may have been true for you when you were young, but I'd say a week is more reasonable."

"If you take things slow, how will you ever keep up with the hustle and bustle of the big city? I hear city folk are always in a hurry!"

"R-right...I'll do my best!"

Lloyd's voice broke a bit at the end, and someone in the crowd yelled, "Don't start crying!" Warm smiles flashed all around.

"Oh, I almost forgot. Lloyd! When ya get to the capital, ask for the Witch of the East Side. Show her this crystal, and she'll help you out." Alka handed him a crystal the size of his fist, and Lloyd stuffed it in his knapsack.

"Thanks, Chief," he said, smiling. "And thanks, everyone. All right, I'd better get going!"

He headed off down the mountain path, stopping often to look behind him at the crowd. Seeing this, his grandfather got nervous all over again.

"*Sigh*... Is that kid really gonna be all right?"

"'Course he will," Alka said, accidentally slipping out truth before she winced, feigned a coughing fit, and ordered, "Never mind! Everyone, back to work!"

She hustled the crowd back inside, thinking, *Boy isn't the least bit weak! He's just surrounded by even stronger people. This journey oughtta give him a little confidence. And then...*

Alka looked back in the direction he'd gone. Lloyd was out of sight now. A warm spring breeze brushed past her cheeks, and she narrowed her eyes at the mountains in the distance.

For the sake of my heart, I need ya to become a great soldier, my beloved Lloyd...

This was the town of Kunlun, the village that stood at the very edge of the world.

After the legendary heroes had saved the planet, they'd departed for distant lands and settled down to make peaceful lives for themselves here. Everyone in the village descended from them. And in that extraordinary village, the feeblest, most earnest boy...was Lloyd Belladonna.

This is a story about that boy. The misunderstandings that arose around him weave this tale together. And if I was to describe the plot with our current cultural zeitgeist in mind, well, I'd say...this is the story of what happens when a kid from the last dungeon boonies moves to a starter town.

To begin, let's discuss the setting—the Kingdom of Azami.

This kingdom was located on the southern end of the continent, blessed with a temperate climate. It faced an ocean filled with the bounty of the seas, and it had access to a great river that crossed the continent, making transport of goods considerably easier than neighboring countries.

Fueled by trade, Azami was divided into five major districts: The Central District, or the place for the royal castle and noble estates, as well as where the army was stationed. The North Side—more or less the kingdom's front door and the location of all kinds of shops. The West Side, a tidy residential district. The South Side, which was nearest to the harbor or the heart of commerce, lively in a very different way from the North Side.

And finally, the East Side, where Lloyd was headed. This was, to be blunt, where the dregs of society gathered.

The East Side was inside the kingdom, but public order was low enough it could hardly be considered part of said territory. An unkempt district with all sorts of things shoved in it—kind of like a dresser stuffed to the brim in a vain attempt to impress a surprise visitor. Half the district was lower- and middle-class homes, but the farther inside, the more it became another world, where all kinds of people ran things according to their own laws.

Paving stones with cracks ignored for years, wooden price tags on garbage (or was it merchandise?) under the awnings of homes, women well past their primes—verging on old—chattering with one another and showing excessive amounts of skin... A run-down vibe welcomed all who came. Lloyd was roaming these backroads late at night, with the little knapsack clearly marking him as a country bumpkin, as he searched for his destination.

Walking an alley with his appearance, he was practically begging to get mugged. A pair of hardworking delinquents quickly approached him, making threats as they leered at him.

But Lloyd didn't even seem to notice. He just breezed right past them.

"Ignoring us, huh? Then we'll just have to get rough."

The leader slammed his shoulder into Lloyd. A classic technique. An unexpected shoulder bump followed by...

"Aughhhhh! That huuuurts!" The delinquent made a big show.

"Wh-what?! You'll pay for this, kid!" And his partner took advantage of that to press the kid for a payout.

Be careful of this scam if you ever find yourself in a seedy part of town!

Accosted by this thug, Lloyd looked terribly surprised. "Huh?"

"'Huh,' what? You messed up my buddy's shoulder!"

"Ow! That seriously hurts! Call a doctor! I think it's broken!"

"But I barely bumped into you!"

"Doctor! Doctor!" he chanted, sweating profusely, and crumpled over.

The man's performance (?) was certainly convincing.

"Man, he's really going for it today," his partner muttered under his breath, impressed, before zeroing in on Lloyd again. "Like hell you did! You're paying for his medical bills! Pay up! All the money you got! Everything on you! Leave it all here! And no, you can't keep your underwear, either!"

"A doctor...," the injured man hissed as his coconspirator got more and more worked up.

His friend broke off his demands, gradually realizing his injured partner wasn't faking it. "Huh? Uh...you mean...for real?"

"For real!" he shrieked. "Can't you see it swelling up, you numbskull? Get a damn doctor! ...Oh shit. This is real bad!"

His friend stared at him a moment, then turned back to Lloyd with eyes even more bloodshot than before. "Yo! Look what you did to him! You'll pay for this, kid!"

"Uh... That's exactly what you said a moment ago..."

"Shut the hell up! This time I *really* mean it! We gotta get him to a doctor   stat! Stop dickin' around! Hand it over!"

He held a hand out expectantly, but Lloyd looked lost.

Um...hand it over? ...What exactly? Uh... Is he asking for a high five?

Not knowing what else to do, he lightly tapped the delinquent's hand. Or at least...to Lloyd, it was a limp slap. But you guessed it...

A loud crunch rang through the alley. His "lightly slapped" hand rocketed from place, winding around his shoulder three times before he hit the ground in a crash landing.

"Aiiiieeee!"

Now it was the friend's turn to writhe in the middle of the street, his hand and shoulder twisted in unnatural angles. Both of them were coated in mud.

"Uh? Really? But that was the lightest of high fives!"

The delinquent's reactions definitely seemed to be more than just "dramatic," and Lloyd was thoroughly rattled. But when he stepped closer out of concern, they scuttled away like a pair of cockroaches.

"W-we'll remember... I mean, no! Please forget this ever happened!"

The pair were too cowed to even finish delivering this classic line—used to save face by fleeing cowards everywhere—as they staggered away, leaning on each other for support.

"Huh...I wonder if that was some sort of street performance? I've heard they have those in the big city."

Baffled, Lloyd tried to explain this away by attributing it to life in the "big city," a magic phrase that seemed to solve everything, even though it was a stretch this time.

As he continued to shake his head in bewilderment, he found his way to a store on a gentle slope of a hill. There were a number of old potion pots hanging from the eaves, and a shoddy small sign that announced WE'VE GOT POTIONS, as if it'd been posted to keep up appearances. The whole vibe was so phony that it actually made it seem like a *real* witch's shop.

"So this is where the Witch of the East Side lives."

The door was so rickety that he was almost afraid to knock on it, but there was a light spilling softly out from under it. Certain there was someone home, Lloyd opened the door, softly calling out as he did.

"Hello?"

The rusted hinges made the door rather heavy. Behind it was a woman wearing a black robe; a wide-brimmed, pointy hat; and rimless glasses—looking every bit the part of a witch. She had flaxen hair and was in the middle of reading a book, a cup of coffee in her free hand. She looked to be about Lloyd's age, but something about her air made her seem much older.

The shop interior was also extremely befitting of a witch—with half-made potions, mortars, unfamiliar and poisonous-looking thorny plants, and piles of old tomes in the corners as if specifically trying to create that mood.

"........."

She lowered the thick volume in her hand, gave him a disinterested look-over, and then went back to her book. The ensuing silence was broken only by the sound of the page turning.

Her utter lack of response left Lloyd unsure what to do next, so he just kind of stood there. Perhaps this was what wore her down eventually.

She hooked her shoulder-length hair over one ear and said, "What?" The voice emerged from deep within her chest, which he could tell was impressive even under her loose robes.

"Er, um…I was told to come see the Witch of the East Side."

"Hmph. You have a message from someone?"

"Uh, no. I'm not a messenger, I'm…"

"Oh, so you're someone who *knows* I'm a witch." She took a sip of coffee, closed her book, and glared at him from behind her glasses. "Do you know what it means for a child like you to ask a favor of a witch?"

This sounded so ominous that Lloyd flinched. "No, I was just told to come here."

The witch sighed, shaking her head.

"According to tradition, witches grant wishes in exchange for payment of equal value," she explained. "You must be ready to make a sacrifice. With that in mind, what is it you wish for? Marie the Witch will guide your path, no matter how impossible the task—just make sure you don't regret it."

This was more a threat than anything else. Lloyd swallowed hard, working up the nerve to proceed.

"I-I've come from the country to become a soldier! Can I stay here until then?"

There was a long pause, then she coughed. "According to tradition…"

"Yeah, um, I've already heard your spiel."

"Then go find an inn and look at some job postings in the town square, ya little shit!"

Her theatrical shtick instantly shattered into pieces. She'd jumped out of her chair, looking like a girl scolding her bratty kid brother. Lloyd cowered slightly.

"Geez," she grumbled. "What do you think witches are? Handymen? Charity workers? Hospitality staff? Is that what they're teaching kids these days? Where did you even come from?!"

"Uh, a town called Kunlun…"

"Yeah, yeah. Well, go back to there and tell them witches aren't… Hmm? Hold up. Kunlun?"

The witch sat back down and stroked her chin on her hand, as if trying to remember something. And a moment later, the color drained from her face, making her look like someone who'd forgotten something really important at home.

"Uh…boy…what's the name of your village chief?"

"Hmm? Alka. Is there a problem?"

At the mention of that name, the witch's back snapped as straight as a stick, and sweat began pouring down from every pore on her face. She clasped her hands and positioned them on the tops of her tights, prim and proper like a job applicant at an interview.

She was muttering something under her breath. It sounded like an incantation. "No, it could be just someone with the same name. I mean, what could she possibly want after all this time…?"

Lloyd watched this for a moment, then exclaimed, "Oh, I totally forgot!" He undid the knot on his knapsack and began rummaging around inside. "She said to show you this…"

He gingerly put a huge hunk of crystal down on the table.

"My hopes are dashed! It's definitely her!" The witch threw her arms up like an athlete who'd missed a goal.

Lloyd smiled in response, misreading her actions as part of her great sense of humor.

The witch saw him looking, snatched her hat off, ruffled her flaxen hair, and started briskly making more coffee without a single trace of her dismissive attitude from earlier.

"Where are my manners?" she asked. "And? She didn't give you any sort of message for me? Oh god, she didn't come here with you, did she? That'd be too much for me to—"

"No, no messages. And it's just me."

When she heard this last part, the witch pumped her fist, shouting triumphantly. "Yee, boi!" She was totally acting her age now.

Hand still clenched, she shot Lloyd a look and asked, "Uh, so you're seriously just…planning to stay here instead of an inn?"

"Sh-she said if I showed you the crystal, you'd understand…"

Both pairs of eyes turned toward it. In the next instant, a stream of aurora-esque light shot out of the rock, forming the shape of a person.

As the outline grew clearer, Lloyd recognized her—it was the chief

of Kunlun, Alka herself. But when the witch saw that petite body and those distinctive twin pigtails, she let out a little shriek and instantly fell on her hands and knees.

She rubbed her forehead into the floor as she begged, "Please, show mercy!" several times.

Just as it seemed like the floor was about to start smoking from the friction, Alka finally began to speak. "Howdy. Long time no see, Marie. It's your master, Alka! Remember me?!"

"Eep."

Whatever "traditions yada yada yada" monologue she'd made sound so imposing had gone straight out the window.

"I reckon it's a bit much to ask ya for a favor after all these years, but my precious, *precious* young'un, Lloyd, has said he wants to be a soldier... I'm sure he'll get in, but take care of him until then, ya hear?"

"Eep... I-if I may be so bold," the witch said, head still firmly planted on the ground. Her boobs smothered the floor. "I do have a few questions..."

"Oh, I almost forgot. This message is just a recordin' so I can't answer any questions! Sorry!"

To that, the witch instantly yelled, "You really had me going there, pip-squeak! Glad to see you still haven't gotten any taller!" She leaped to her feet, grinning wildly, and slapped the crystal across its smooth surface a few times as she cackled.

And the moment the "recording" saw how her attitude changed, Alka grinned, looking right at her. "I figured if I said that you'd screw up, Marie."

"Eep!"

Black cape fluttering, the witch slammed her entire body onto the floor to grovel—more like "eat *gravel*"—forehead pressed flat on the ground. Alka watched this with an icy smile, then seemed to lose interest quickly.

"Anyhow, I do always enjoy seeing you make a purdy fool of yourself, but...either way, I'd appreciate your help. Even if he does somehow fail the test, I'm sure you'll take care of it, Marie. See ya! …Oh and, Lloyd! If ya get lonely, I'll pop over and rock ya to sleep anytime!"

And with that, the image scattered into particles of light, leaving Lloyd gaping and the witch crushed. Quite a bizarre sight, indeed.

The idea of her rocking him to sleep had Lloyd blushing. Meanwhile, the witch slowly clambered back to her feet. She looked even more embarrassed than Lloyd.

She straightened her garment out, ran her fingers through her hair to remove any hints of dust, adjusted her glasses, cleared her throat, and screeched, "Goddamn herrrrr! I thought I was finally free! You can't just pop up with weird favors, *loli* Grandma! *Loli* Grammmmaaa!"

Then she hurled the crystal into a closet and slammed the door as hard as she could. Not one for taking care of her home, it seemed.

Breathing heavily, she saw Lloyd awkwardly staring at her and regained some of her composure. She sat down again.

"*Huh*… W-well, if it's her asking, I've got no choice. I'll look after you until this test thing, um…"

"Oh, I'm Lloyd. Lloyd Belladonna."

"Okay, Lloyd. I'm Marie. They call me the Witch of the East Side."

"Uh, sorry, I guess? I know this is a lot. I'll help in any way I can!"

His earnest frown seemed to drain the spite from Marie.

"No need for any of that," she said in a much nicer tone this time. "I've got a spare room in back. You can put your things there. Since I wasn't expecting company, it's not clean or anything, so we'll have to clear out the mess now. Otherwise, it's so late, you'll never get a chance to sleep. Just shove it all in a corner or something." She pointed to a room in back.

"Sure thing!"

Lloyd grabbed his knapsack and headed back. As he passed Marie, he flashed her another gentle smile. "Thanks for everything!"

What a well-mannered kid.

Meanwhile, Marie had come to the sudden realization that her new roomie was a boy. And they were the same age to boot.

Staring after him, she muttered, "Seems awful nice for someone from Kunlun...or anyone connected to that *loli* grandma...surprisingly so."

She took a sip of her coffee. It'd gone cold.

"Well, my master's always had two or three screws loose," she mumbled to herself. She picked up her book, thumbing through the pages since she'd neglected to use a bookmark. "Now, where was I...?"

"By the way," added Alka, stepping out of the closet. The real one, not a projection this time. "If ya dare lay a finger on my darlin' little boy, I'll make sure ya live out the rest of yer days as a frog!"

"Pfftt!"

Forget finding her place in the book. A massive spray of brown liquid made it impossible to tell what was written on the page at all.

"Why were you in my closet?!" Marie yelled, dribbling coffee from her nose.

Alka didn't appear at all sorry. "Mm? Well, obviously, I teleported here usin' that crystal as a gate."

"Oh, I wish you wouldn't go around using techniques that go beyond human limitations! That much never changes! And geez, I'm not going after a boy I just met!"

"Hmm? Is that so?"

"Of course! What do you think I am?!"

Alka snorted. "Look at yourself! I know ya spent hours dithering outside that host club before eventually giving up! You have virgin written all over ya!"

"I am not a...w-wait, how do you know that?! What?! Are you watching me?! You knew where I was?"

"I'll give ya credit for stopping yourself, at least. It seems you haven't entirely forgotten your position. That's why I'm trustin' him to ya. Thanks, Marie."

"...Happy to help," Marie said mechanically through gritted teeth, wearing an expression like she'd just taken a huge chomp into a bug. No, that's too mild—it was like she'd bitten into a bug, and its scraggly leg had lodged itself into her gums.

Now that she'd aired everything out, Alka started burrowing back into the closet. She paused, talking to Marie with her back still turned.

"Oh, yes, yes. As punishment for callin' me a *loli* grandma, I've placed a mild curse wishing misfortune on you in ancient runes."

"Whyyyy?! You can't use the wisdom of yore for petty grievances!"

But even as she protested…

Thunk!

"Ouch!"

Marie stubbed her toe on the table leg. Alka laughed so hard there were tears welling in her eyes, and then she vanished into the closet.

Thoroughly defeated, Marie collapsed on the table, swearing under her breath until she fell asleep.

With the wood grain of the table imprinted on half her face, Marie woke to the sound of a rhythmic tapping. Annoyed by the sun streaming through her shabby window, she narrowed her eyes, looking around.

"Hmm mm-hmm mm-hmm mm-mm-mm-mm-mmaa-aaah!"

The would-be soldier from the night before was standing in the kitchen, humming to himself, chopping greens like he'd done it his whole life. He tossed them into a pot on the stove top.

"Oh…I guess I drifted off…"

She sat up, her chair creaking…and a blanket slid off her. Just as Marie realized the boy must have put it on her, he heard her moving and turned with a smile in her direction.

"Good morning! Sorry to take over your kitchen like this."

"Mornin'…uh, I don't mind. Thanks for the blanket."

"I thought about carrying you to your room, but I figured better not to go in a lady's room without permission…"

This reminded Marie that her bedroom was less befitting her status as a lady than as a resident of the totally trashed East Side, and she was instantly relieved he hadn't seen it.

"Quite a gentleman," she remarked to hide this reaction. She fixed her flaxen hair up with her fingers and took a closer look at what Lloyd was fixing for breakfast.

"Just a moment," he soothed, as if he were trying to placate a child who was begging for a taste test. "I'll have some pancakes ready in a minute."

He put a frying pan on the stove, threw a little oil into the pan, poured in the batter, and flipped over the pancakes. The smell of it got her appetite going, and Marie put plates and honey on the table, moving so snappily you'd never imagine she'd just woken up a moment earlier.

The pancakes were served along a chicken broth with greens in it, a breakfast that left Marie speechless.

"Sorry that it's a simple meal."

"…Not at all."

Anyone living alone knows that waking up to breakfast is, like, the ultimate joy in life. Especially after a night of getting worked over by her former master—who might not have had horns or a club but was otherwise indistinguishable from a demon. This boy's consideration and the scent of the broth wormed their way into her heart.

"You can stay here as long as you like."

"Huh?"

"Uh, never mind. Time to dig in!"

Marie took an enormous bite of her pancakes. She'd slapped quite a bit of honey on it and stuffed her cheeks so full she looked like a chipmunk. Then she washed it down with a few gulps of soup.

"Amazing! I haven't eaten anything not from a can in so long!"

"Er…? From a can?"

"Yeah…I'm a witch, you see," she attempted to explain away.

The Witch of the East Side seemed to be raising her middle finger to the age-old public image of witches. After devouring three giant pancakes, she made a big show of elegantly making more coffee.

Seeing the look of satisfaction on her face, Lloyd smiled gently and began cleaning up. Meanwhile, as Maire was faced with this entirely unsoldierly display of good housekeeping skills, she asked the obvious question.

"Uh...Lloyd, do you actually want to be a soldier?"

"Uh, yes... Sorry," Lloyd said, turning to face her as he dried off a plate. He bowed his head slightly in apology.

"Oh, don't... No need to apologize."

Then Marie remembered that this boy was from Kunlun. "That was a stupid question," she reflected. How could she forget that? As he did the dishes, she began filling him in on the test.

"The general admissions test to the military academy in the Kingdom of Azami is in the middle of the month, so it's still a ways off. You know what it involves?"

"Um, I heard there was a combat test, a written test on magic, and an interview?"

"Yes...they change it up a little each time, but basically that. The combat test is the most important by far."

"*Sigh*, I thought so..."

"I mean, they know we all have our strengths and weaknesses with magic, so as long as you know the basics, that's enough. Plus, a soldier's work is mostly guarding and heavy lifting. They need strong men."

"Urp."

"And lately, the man in charge, Colonel Merthophan, is really going for it, recruiting all over...there's no set limit to how many cadets they accept, but there's a lot of competition for those slots."

Marie went on about intel she'd received as of late. "The eldest boy from the heavily decorated Lidocaine family. And the rumored Belt Princess. And that infamous female mercenary..."

But coming from the very edge of the continent, Lloyd had never heard of any of them.

"You sure know a lot," he commented.

"That's 'cause I'm a witch...but really, running a shop like this, you tend to hear things. Especially here on the East Side: Nobody has any money, so they pay for potions with information." Marie proudly took a sip of her coffee.

On the other side of the conversation, Lloyd was looking increasingly gloomy. "I was afraid it was all about strength...never been my strong suit."

Coffee cup still held up to her lips, Marie's brows twitched. Then she gave Lloyd a look of skepticism.

"What are you talking about? You're from Alka's village! You oughtta be more worried about the interview and, like, common sense."

"No...I've really never been very strong." Lloyd hung his head, scratching his cheek. "I mean, it took me six whole days to get here."

Marie had no idea what he was talking about. It'd taken him six days to get here from that remote area, hopping carriages and trains? How did that have anything to do with his physical prowess?

Ha-ha-ha...he doesn't mean he walked here in six days, right? That would be ridiculous.

As she chuckled to herself, she took another sip of coffee.

"No! He's totally serious!"

Another spray of brown liquid. Without bothering to mop it up, she turned on Lloyd, desperate not to believe it.

"You mean by train, right?" she demanded.

"Huh? No, I ran the whole way. But you're right, six days is a really long time...my grandfather said two would be plenty."

A silence settled over the room.

"No, no, no, no! Lloyd! You're crazy strong!"

"Er...thanks for the encouragement. Everyone always says I've got guts, at least, but I know better than anyone how weak I am."

Marie looked at him like he must be joking, but the boy himself was clearly genuinely worried, and she'd spent enough time in the information trade to tell if someone was lying or not.

And it's not a lie...which means he really doesn't...

The outer realms...the weakest boy from Kunlun...by the standards of a town that made common sense evaporate like morning mist.

As if making sure...or perhaps trying to get through to him, Marie said, "But on the way here, you certainly must have met a monster or two. There must be all kinds of dangerous monsters on the road. If you can beat them, you're definitely pretty strong."

"No, I was really lucky. I never crossed paths with any of them."

"...Right."

"But there were lots of animals! Big locusts, fire-breathing lizards..."

"Those are clearly monsters! And really dangerous ones at that!"

Lloyd clearly took this as a joke and laughed it off. "Ah-ha-ha, I think I can tell the difference between animals and monsters. Monster are all, you know, 'The world belongs to us!' and they always have a second and third form..."

At this spine-chilling declaration, Marie deflated, collapsing on the table.

Lord! How could you send this kid to the capital, loli *Grandma? He's too much!*

She considered giving him a long lecture on common sense and the definition of monsters, but he was so clearly well-meaning, earnest, and genuinely convinced that he was weak, she couldn't find any way to broach this topic.

"The only thing I'm really good at is housework... They say I'm the best in the village at cleaning!"

"At cleaning...cleaning what? Cleaning up after your enemies? Disposing of corpses of invaders?"

"Enemies? Corpses? Nope, just normal cleaning."

At this, Marie glanced toward the kitchen. It'd been buried deep in empty cans, bottles, and scraps left over from potions—forming a mini–East Side all on its own.

But move that bus! Now that Lloyd had plowed through it, it was so clean that it sparkled in the sunlight.

A wimpy, kind homemaker, huh... I can see why the master's paying extra attention to him. He's totally her type.

Putting the matter of Alka's preferences aside, Marie honestly admitted his work on her kitchen was amazing.

"Oh, it's nothing," he said, sheepishly modest but clearly pleased. He was certainly confident in this area. "Eh-heh-heh. There's a trick to it, you see."

"Oh yeah? Like a cleaning hack?"

"More or less, yeah."

Marie definitely wanted to know more, so she came over and stood next to him, staring at his hands. Lloyd whipped out a rag like a salesman doing a demonstration of his product.

"See this rag right here?"

"Mm-hmm?"

"There's an ancient rune stitched into it, so anything you wipe with it gets super clean."

"Cleaning hack, my ass!"

She hadn't expected the wisdom of the ancients to be applied to good housekeeping. Her reaction was super loud, and Lloyd was so surprised, he went back to looking really anxious.

"I-is that bad?"

"It's not bad except for in all the ways it is!"

And with that, Marie began thumping her head on the wall.

And it's the disenchant *rune! I had to labor under Alka for* years *before I was able to learn that thing!*

Even as Marie was hammering her head on the wall like a professional construction worker, Lloyd accidentally struck one final blow.

"I don't really get it, but apparently a side effect is that it gets rid of any grime or dirt!"

"A side effect! All my work for a friggin' side effect!"

This was too much for Marie, and she collapsed against the wall, tears in her eyes. If she were to hear it'd only taken Lloyd three months to acquire this rune, she'd definitely have pounded a head-sized hole in her wall.

But Lloyd had no idea how to handle this situation, so he just apologized.

"I'm sorry… I know, it's nothing impressive. This and a spell to make it rain are all I can really…"

There goes that head-sized hole.

"I knew it... Common sense has no bearing on anyone from that stupid village..."

Several days had passed since Lloyd started staying at the witch's shop.

Well, she called it a shop...but it wasn't like she had anything ready for sale. It was more like neighbors stopped by to chat and picked up some medicine while they were there.

As a result, it was pretty much always open. Since business revolved entirely around Marie, Lloyd mostly focused on cleaning and laundry or going shopping for her. Even in the capital, he was the World's Best Wife.

One day, while Lloyd was out shopping, a local master carpenter stopped by.

"All done, Marie!"

With practiced ease, his thin and wrinkled arms had hammered up the repairs to the hole in her wall, and he was already putting his tools away.

"Thanks so much," Marie replied.

"Not a problem! You've given my wife free medicine often enough. Time we paid you back. But how'd this even happen, eh? Somethin' smash into it?"

"Ah-ha-ha...never mind that. I made some tea, if you want to rest a bit. You're not getting any younger."

"Don't mind if I do," he said, settling down. He knocked the tea back in one gulp. "Damn, that's good! Been a while since I had any tea. Tea leaves have been so expensive lately, we've just been drinking hot water."

"Oh, I know. I got lucky and stocked up before the price jumped. But I wonder why it's gone up so much."

Not just luxury items—the prices for foodstuff across the board had been rising bit by bit, and Marie hadn't heard a single good reason.

The tea had made the carpenter talkative, and he had a lot to share.

"Well, what I hear is, there was a rockslide on the road to the west. You know the one; all the merchants used it. Totally cut it off."

According to his sources, this had happened several days before, blocking imports.

"With that road closed, the wagons would have to go the long way around," Marie added.

"And not just that! Even if they loop around to the central road, there's been these locust monsters plaguing the area, so it's not worth the risk. Right now, all we can get in the markets is stuff from the Jiou Empire."

"I see... That explains the price."

In recent years, relations between the Kingdom of Azami and the Jiou Empire had become strained, which meant their merchants would seize this chance to jack their prices way up.

"Uh-huh, and some folks are speculatin' the Jiou Empire were the ones that blew that road up. Maybe even released those monsters... One of them giant locusts even showed up in town! That would never have happened a few years ago. What are the guards doing?"

"...Hard to know what any administration is thinking," Marie commented, pretending to be totally engrossed in this conversation. She took another sip of tea.

"Anyway, long story short, more and more of our merchants are starting to hope for a war. The king's been pushing for one for a while, and with them backing him...well, it's bad news for everyone else."

Listening to the carpenter ramble, Marie was starting to realize that this chain of events couldn't be a coincidence.

A rockslide, a monster outbreak, war...is the Jiou Empire really behind all this?

While Marie was lost in thought, the carpenter continued railing against the royal family.

"When was the last time the royals did anything for us? They let the East Side get festered with crime! You know about that new statue of the king in the Central District? The one that's all perfectly proportioned and shit? I mean, have you *seen* the guy? He's on the chubby side! And if you've got time to make something like that, hire more guards!"

"I agree. It looks nothing like him."

"And the princess disappeared years ago. What is this country coming to...? But I guess there's no point running your ear off about it, ha-ha-ha."

He got up, telling her, "Call me if you need anything else!" and gave her a big wave. As he opened the door, he found a sweet-looking boy—Lloyd—carrying a bundle of goods.

"I'm back! Oh? Are you a carpenter? What brings you here?"

Lloyd set a large sack down on the floor and then clasped his hands in front of him as he gave the carpenter a polite bow.

"Hello, son. I was just repairing Marie's wall for her. For free."

"F-for free? Are you sure?"

The carpenter rubbed his nose, puffing his chest up. "This job's no big deal! And Marie's been a big help to me and mine. Never hesitates to share potions with us poor folk. She's our savior! Yeah! The Savior of the East Side! Legends about our hero will traverse the continent someday!"

"Savior? I *knew* she was a good person!"

All this praise was too much for Marie, who turned bright red. "Hey!" she yelped. "I didn't do anything special! I got information in return! It's a fair exchange! I'm no savior, and I won't allow anything to go beyond this house!"

The carpenter gave a hearty chuckle and left, this time for good. To dispel some of her bashfulness, Marie cleared her throat.

"*Ahem!* Argh...so, Lloyd, I'm assuming you got the shopping done?" she asked, sounding a bit like a fussy older sister.

She had reason to be concerned. Part of the reason she'd sent Lloyd out on a shopping run was so this boy from a place as outlandish as Kunlun could start getting used to how things worked in the normal parts of the world.

If he just damaged some property, that's one thing. But if he hurt anyone, I'll have to call the loli *grandma and make her go heal them...I mean, she did say she can heal anything short of a carcass. Argh, a* carcass. *That phrasing makes me shudder…*

Meanwhile, Lloyd started to show off the results of his excursion with a charming little grin.

"Uh, yeah! You needed a wooden pestle, a mortar, some flour…oh, and look! I brought a small souvenir, too."

"A souvenir?"

She'd been eyeing that giant sack since he set it down, and he unlaced it to reveal that it was…packed full of tea leaves. One look at the color and she could tell this was some top-class stuff. A pleasant smell wafted off the heap.

There was far too much of it to count as *a small souvenir*…especially since they'd just been talking about how expensive tea was these days.

Marie frowned for a moment and then finally dared to ask, "…What is this?"

"Oh, some tea leaves I got from a farmer across the western mountains. As a token of his thanks!"

Huh? I thought everyone was panicking about the rockslide there…

Marie was too preoccupied wondering why a farmer mixed up in that mess would ever give this much tea away to question what he was thanking Lloyd for. Was this some sort of scam?

Her voice was tinged with skepticism. "A farmer from the west came all the way to Azami?"

Lloyd was the one who looked surprised this time. "Huh? No."

"What?"

This conversation wasn't adding up.

Flustered, Lloyd started babbling, spewing some incredibly absurd claims.

"Like I said, I got it from a farmer to the west. I went shopping at a village two mountains over. The flour was cheaper there. And on the way…"

"……………*Two mountains?!* What?! You went that far *to shop*?!"

"Mm? Sure, it's a short walk! Don't you usually go that far to buy things?"

Bam! And Marie slammed her head into the freshly patched wall again. The carpenter had done an excellent job, and it was completely undamaged. Marie's forehead, less so.

As the polished wall gleamed, so did the tears welling up in her eyes. Internally, she was shrieking. *Okay, fine. I admit, I didn't specifically tell him that he had to do his shopping inside the country borders, but—!*

(Side note: A shopping trip in Kunlun means going to a village three or four mountains away. A round trip that would take most people days but the villagers only an hour.)

Marie was still wrestling with the philosophical definition of "a shopping run" when Lloyd delivered his final blow.

"Oh, the road there was packed! Seemed like this rockslide was totally blocking off the road, so I went ahead and moved all the debris out of the way, and the workers were all, 'You're a god!' and handed me some freshly picked tea leaves. I got the flour for basically nothing, too. Like I'm a god! So silly."

"*...Uh-huh. Yep. Sure.*"

"I mean, it only took me like an hour to shift it all to the side of the road! The chief would have just cast a recovery spell and fixed it in a second. Man, city folks really do know how to butter you up!"

Clutching her head, Marie managed to say, "Next time, try shopping inside the country. Lloyd...there's a lot you need to understand. But first..."

He must have taken that as a prelude to a scolding, because he quickly hung his head.

"S-sorry! You said I could keep the change, but it was too much, right?"

"No, that's not what I'm trying to..."

"I know I should probably have brought back the leftover cash, but...I used it for this."

Lloyd sheepishly took an elegant brooch out of his pocket—a very intricate one at that. An amber tortoiseshell and the generous use of silver accents made it clear that this piece was very expensive.

"What is that?"

"Oh, a present."

"For who?"

"For you, Marie."

Marie stared at the brooch for a long time, repeating, "For who?"

"Like I said, for you. You're letting me stay here for free, and I didn't think a little housework here and there made up for that in any way."

He held out the brooch with a smile that didn't display any ulterior motives. Marie was forced to bashfully take it from him, muttering, "Thanks."

...I've got to teach him some common sense, stat. Not just how far to go for shopping...I've got to find a way to explain how loaded it is to get a girl any kind of gift.

To be honest, Marie was downright unsettled by how happy it had made her. She quickly pinned it to her chest and took a look at it in the mirror, realizing for the second time that this was clearly worth a lot.

"...This is really well crafted. Definitely not a knockoff, either."

"Oh, well, you see, on my way, I found a merchant who was upset because the river had dried up; they couldn't get their ship through, so I made it rain for him; and he was so happy, he insisted I take the most expensive item on him, but I didn't think it was right to take it for free, so I gave him all the money I had left over for it."

He's managed to solve inflation in our kingdom just by running errands?!

No one else could cure a nation's economic woes in a single shopping trip. Marie shook her head.

"These damn Kunlun villagers!" she wailed.

And Lloyd's little excursion had saved not only the country but the fate of a certain girl.

That girl was Selen Hemein, the daughter of a local lord. She was staying at an inn at the capital, passing time until the admissions test. Her temporary residence was near the East Side—a simple place, mostly used by merchants who just needed a place to sleep.

It was absolutely not the sort of place designed for long-term stays, but she had her reasons for being there: to avoid attracting any unwanted attention. A run-down place spared her that, making it far more comfortable for her and then some.

There was just one problem: The place didn't offer meals. Most inns had communal kitchens available if you wanted to slap something together, but she'd never cooked before.

On her way here, she'd lived on dehydrated rice that she didn't even bother to rehydrate, choosing to wash it down with a few swigs of water. Her hunger levels were already pretty far past their limit. So she pulled her hood all the way down over her eyes, driven forward by the rumble of her stomach, and reluctantly headed for the city market.

Noon on the South Side meant it was teeming with adventurers, merchants, and tourists, all shopping at the market, and the sheer bustle of the place was starting to overwhelm her. Everywhere Selen looked, there were people, people, and more people, and she began to feel nauseous looking at their bobbing heads.

"Maybe I should have waited until evening..."

But the distressed whimpers in her belly wouldn't hear anything of it. At least the noise of the busy streets drowned out these loud rumbles.

Selen clamped her hand on her stomach, scanning the area to see if any stalls caught her eye. But with so many shops to choose from, she ended up getting swept along by the crowd, unable to make an executive decision.

"...Hah...hah..."

She was breathing heavily now, far more exhausted than she'd been on the trip here, even though she hadn't done anything worth noting. Then she caught a whiff of a fragrant scent from behind her.

When she whipped around, she found a stall selling fried chicken. Large plates were piled high with wild vegetables and little river fish. The smell of hot oil was making people stop in their tracks and buy the deep-fried food wrapped in paper, lightly salted, and eaten standing up.

The prospect of hot food for the first time in days made Selen's mouth water.

Anyone else would have immediately stepped forward, but Selen had never bought anything for herself, not even food. She had the money, but she was so nervous about the whole affair that she just stood there, compulsively checking her wallet for the umpteenth time.

"...Hmm..."

She peered past her hood, observing how people purchased the food and running through the encounter in her mind, like someone working up the nerve to step into an upscale hair salon for the first time.

She waited until the floor of customers had died down a little, saw her chance to buy in peace, and just as she was about to step forward...

"Excuse me. A word?"

A hand on her shoulder made her spin around.

Two soldiers stood behind her in dark green uniforms emblazoned with the crest of Azami. They bowed, wearing twin grimaces.

Selen's nervous disposition had attracted their attention.

"Sorry for the inconvenience," one said in a tone all business. "But we'll need to see some ID. With the foundation-day festival approaching, there are many suspicious types around, you see...enemy agents releasing monsters on the streets and the like."

Selen finally figured it out.

"...You think I'm one of those shady characters?"

She could certainly see why someone wearing a hood on a warm spring day would pique their interest. She sighed, realizing she could hardly blame them.

Growing impatient, the soldier behind the officious one spoke up harshly. "Don't go telling us your appearance isn't obviously suspicious, now. If you've got nothing to hide, take that hood off."

She slapped his hand away as he reached for it, but in that split second, he caught a glimpse of the face glaring up at him.

Her face was wrapped in a leather belt, dyed a sinister bloodred. The belt wound around her head this way and that way, and one eye gazed out from a gap.

The soldier's voice trembled. "Th-the Belt Princess..."

"From the central region? I guess she really did come to enlist."

The first guy sounded like he'd seen a ghost. Selen always hated this part the most. She gritted her teeth, her glare becoming all the more hostile. This unnerved the two soldiers so much that they began to attract a small crowd. Had they heard the words *belt princess*? She could feel them staring even under her hood.

"............"

Selen hastily walked away, unable to bear it any longer, continuing to ignore the calls of the soldiers as she headed away from the crowds. All the while, she muttered angrily to herself, heedless of how suspicious that made her seem.

"…I didn't do anything wrong! And they treat me like a criminal…"

People called her the Cursed Belt Princess.

This was Selen. She'd been born in the center of the continent to a wealthy merchant family—an aristocrat.

With its fertile green land, gentle rolling plains, and convenient access to the continent's great river, it became prosperous from post-war trade with all sorts of countries, and it soon was a pillar of commerce in the continent. As with any trade hub, strange things naturally found their way there. Her father was a purveyor of such goods, both to aid in negotiations and to please himself.

But this little hobby would dramatically alter the fate of his daughter, Selen.

When she was four, she'd played in her father's treasure room and happened to lay her hands on an ancient item known as the cursed belt—with tragic consequences. A servant had found the stone door to the treasure room open and dashed inside to find…Selen crying in the center of the room with the belt bound tightly around her face.

Her father tried an arsenal of tricks to remove it from her head. But it wouldn't budge one bit. High-ranking monks, merchants from the east, the finest scholars from the royal capital…all of them threw up their hands in despair.

And as time passed, the initial looks of pity she'd received from those around her vanished, and they began to shun her.

The red belt stayed with her as she grew, a crimson bloodstain wrapped around her face, blocking one eye, making her other look increasingly hostile. What had once been beautiful blond hair now poked out from the gaps in the belt like weeds growing through the cracks of an old shack.

In time, she could no longer bear to see how others looked at her, and she seldom left her room. Her only solace had been the words from a high-principled monk: "If you have power greater than the curse, you can free yourself from it."

With this hope in mind, she'd begun to train.

Day after day, she'd spent sweating away in her room, honing her body, eating whatever food was brought to her, training some more. If her hair had grown too long, she'd ruthlessly snip it off herself, caring nothing for her appearance, only her training—and in time, she'd grown so strong that no average warrior could stand against her.

Her rock-hard physique was at odds with her ultra-pale skin, and a dark, baleful eye peered out from the belt wrapped round her head like bandages on a mummy... This appearance led the world to whisper fearfully about the Cursed Belt Princess.

She was now fifteen, and the belt remained stubbornly attached to her face, and when the capital came recruiting soldiers, she'd answered their call, bringing her here...

Unable to bear the curious looks, she'd seized her moment to make a run for it.

"—W-wait!"

Like a slinky feline, Selen vanished down a side road with the body that she'd chiseled to free herself from this curse. She ran down one narrow alley after another until she reached an opening to a different street entirely.

She pulled the hood back over her, clutching her belly again.

"Exerting myself in this condition...I can't...I need food..."

The chicken from earlier filled her mind. She could almost taste it. Her feet carried her forward in search of a similar shop.

At last, she found a shop selling meat on skewers, but still unsure of how things worked, she once again stopped to observe the other customers from the shadows. This time, she kept her distance, hiding behind a pillar a few dozen yards away to avoid raising suspicion from any more patrols.

A few minutes later, a boy in canvas pants and a linen shirt stopped in front of the skewer shop. "Can you fry something up for me? Anything you'd recommend?"

"Sure thing! The chicken breast is top-notch today! The tenders are real good, too!"

"Then lemme get one of those…no, two."

"You got a good appetite on ya, huh? Give me a sec! Comin' right up!"

The owner quickly fried the chicken up, sprinkling them with rock salt before handing them over. The boy smiled as he paid the owner and walked away, a skewer in each hand.

Watching him, Selen muttered to herself, "Hmm. Same way as the last shop. Maybe I'm overthinking this…" She sighed at her own ignorance.

"You want one?"

The boy with the skewers was standing right in front of her.

She froze in surprise. He must have picked up on this, because he kept talking, keeping his tone relaxed.

"Oh, sorry. You were watching me order, right? And I thought you might want something, so…"

"…You saw me?" Selen said, puzzled. "I thought I was being really stealthy."

Her skepticism was understandable. She was this far away from the stall, standing perfectly still in the shadows… She'd avoided contact with many monsters on her way here using this method, so she was pretty confident in her ability to remain undetected. And she'd been on guard, too —but she still hadn't managed to notice him approaching until he was right in front of her. Who was this boy?

Yet, he kept smiling, looking laid-back. "Ah-ha-ha, that's a good one. You're not a woodcutter! Why would you need to conceal yourself?"

Whoever heard of a woodcutter being stealthy?

©Nao Watanuki

She was unaware that his definition of woodcutter was basically a top-class hunter.

Something wasn't adding up here. Selen frowned under her hood. The boy must have sensed her confusion, because he instantly looked sorry.

"Oh, did I overstep my bounds? In that case, sorry to…"

Gurgle!

Before he finished his sentence, Selen's stomach growled.

"…! Th-that was just…" She scrambled to find an appropriate excuse, but he silently held out the skewer.

The scent of the meat and breading whet her appetite. It looked perfectly seasoned, too. She was starving. This was no time to stand on principle.

Selen lowered her eyes, then reached out and took the skewer from him.

"I know how that feels! On my very first shopping trip, I was so scared I was doing it wrong. Back in the boonies where I'm from, we usually barter and trade for what we need…but in the city, you can just relax and act natural. So I'm told anyway."

"R-really? I'm not so good at acting natural…"

"Well, at the very least, they won't be like the craftsman at the dwarf village and come after you with an ax at the slightest offense."

With that horrifying story, the boy happily chomped into his skewer.

Dwarves are from fairy tales! That and the stealthy woodcutters thing… he must be goofing around to help me relax.

He wasn't joking at all—these were all true stories, and he was speaking from experience, going on about how it was important to show respect to the dwarves by looking them in the eye as equals; with elves, it was vital to wear no iron on your person at all… He continued to dole out practical advice, but not only was it of no use to her, it sounded like urban legends. To her ears, it was like giving out help on how to fend off *kuchisake-onna*, a classic figure in Japanese ghost stories with a Glasgow smile, by "throwing some hard candy in her direction and making your getaway while she's busy sucking on it."

At first, Selen had listened with suspicion, but the boy was so obviously trying to be nice to her that she gradually let her guard down. Once she polished off the skewer, she awkwardly expressed her gratitude.

"Um, thanks…I've almost never been shopping, so…this was a big help."

She took out her wallet and tried to offer him some payment, but he shook her off.

"No, no, don't worry about it."

"No, I should…"

"Honestly, I feel like I just got in the way of you practicing how to shop for yourself. I know! You should take that money and go buy a skewer yourself."

"Er, uh…practicing?"

"I know you're nervous. But don't worry. I'll be right here watching."

He was gradually wearing down her resistance to the idea, but somehow it didn't feel like he was pressuring her into it.

He'll be watching…?

It had been a long time since anyone engaged with her in a normal conversation. She was still uneasy, but she nodded and trotted over to the shop.

I should buy a few to pay him back…or maybe it would be better to get something else at another shop?

She let her imagination whisk her away…

But then she saw the soldiers from earlier pushing their way through the crowd—probably looking for her. She'd spotted them first, and her eyes darted around to secure an escape route.

That was when she saw the boy standing behind her. Looking totally relaxed, he was quietly watching over her.

If…if he were to see my face, with this hideous belt…

That kind smile would give way to a look of horror. Selen couldn't bear the thought.

"...There she is!"

She'd hesitated too long. They'd found her.

"Dammit."

She didn't want to ditch the boy, but it would be worse if he knew her true identity. She shot one longing glance his way and then booked it at full speed.

She heard the guards calling after her, but their cries immediately fell out of earshot as she bolted down the alley, trying to shake off the desire to turn back.

At each corner, she slid on the ground to curve around, crouching and bounding in the direction of another alley, her body hunkered down and keeping a low profile. As if driven by a sense of shame about her curse, she went deeper into a complex web of narrow roads.

"............*hah...hah*... Well, at least I got away...but now how do I get back?"

She didn't know her way around here, much less if this was the South or the East Side.

The rusting trash and weeds sprouting in the gaps between buildings suggested this was the East Side, which made getting back to her inn all the more urgent. But before she could, she caught a whiff of a pungent odor. Had someone left some garbage to rot? She clamped a hand over her face, about to leave, when something fluttered down on top of the heaping pile of trash.

With its colorful, translucent wings fluttering, a locust was happily chowing down on garbage. That alone would be unpleasant enough, but the most horrific thing was this locust's size.

It was as tall as a full-grown man and at least four yards long. A locust that size was crawling out from between two buildings.

On second thought, the rotting thing might have been the carcass of a stray dog. Half-eaten, it was now an unrecognizable lump of flesh, but there were definitely patches of animal fur.

And when this locust saw Selen, it scuttled toward her, scraping against the walls of the buildings. She froze for a moment and missed her chance to back away.

"A bug? No…a monster?"

She remembered the soldier saying something about this as she grabbed the hilt of the rapier at her hip, trying to draw her blade.

"*Screeee!*"

Before she could free it from the scabbard fully, the monster lunged at her, screeching.

It was too late. Selen was about to give up hope, when…

Something whizzed past overhead.

The locust was distracted by this new shadow, pausing to take in the situation. And…

"Hokay."

There was a scrunch. The insect's hard body bent out of shape, and the locust's mandibles twisted away. They twitched a few times, feebly.

The shadow—that nice boy from before—had landed on the ground, grabbed the locust by its wings, and tossed it aside like kicking trash to the side of the road.

Thunk.

A dull, heavy noise echoed through the alley—hard to believe that sound came from a bug. The locust's legs folded. It was dead.

Selen could scarcely believe her eyes. Fighting an unknown monster in a narrow alley with no room to maneuver… The situation had been so dangerous, she'd feared for her life. But this boy had dispatched the monster with ease—as if to mock her fears. Her mouth hung open, slack, as she stared at his back and slumped to the ground.

"Are you okay? Are you hurt?" He spoke as if nothing had happened. He held out a hand, his smile as gentle as before.

"I-I'm fine…," Selen said as she took it.

His build was far from that of a hardened warrior's body; these were the kind of muscles that one built from living an ordinary life… It made it even harder to believe he'd been able to beat that monster, and she couldn't conceal her shock.

But this boy's totally normal build, manner, and facial expressions all said he had nothing to hide—that he was just concerned about her well-being.

"Th-thank you," she stammered.

"Did your first attempt at shopping get to be too much? Looked like you panicked and ran off. Don't worry, nobody's gonna throw an ax at you."

He patted her on the shoulder. "It'll be fine!" he said and started brushing the dirt off her clothes.

She was so rattled, she just stood there and let him. And as a result, she failed to stop him from pulling her hood off.

"A-augh!"

Her bound face was exposed. She hastily yanked the hood back up, then stared at the ground, shrinking upon herself, trembling.

...He must be so creeped out.

"Um..."

Not only was this boy not skeeved out, he just pulled her hood off again. With an unchanging smile, he began gently wiping her cheek like he was looking after a small child.

"You've got dirt on your face."

Selen couldn't believe he'd seen her face and not reacted at all.

"Is this the latest fashion trend in the city? I don't really get that stuff..."

(I'm sure you'll all feel the same way once you watch a couture fashion show from another country.)

But Selen was too busy turning bright red to hear a word he'd said.

She stood stunned for a minute and then drew it back over her face—this time to hide her blushing cheeks. Then she looked up at him, meeting his eyes. He grew flustered suddenly, as if he'd just remembered something.

"Oh, I've gotta get home and get supper started! Sorry! I really need to go!"

And off he went.

"Um!" she called after him. "My name's Selen!"

"Oh, uh, cool. I'm Lloyd. See ya!"

With that, the boy—Lloyd—moved like a seasoned parkour artist, kicking off the sides of a wall like he was climbing stairs and vanishing over the other side.

"........."

Selen was left staring after him, still feeling the warm touch of his hand on her cheek.

That evening, Selen was headed back to her inn, arms full of goods.

Even with her hood pulled low, she had a little pep to her step, giving off an upbeat vibe that would have been unthinkable a few hours before—her feet moving around as if she were dancing. She'd gotten carried away and bought a little too much, but she could haul everything without much difficulty.

That was because she had Lloyd's natural smile replaying on an endless loop through her mind.

If I stay in the capital, I'm sure I'll see him again...

The thought brought a smile to her lips. With the belt bound around her face, smiling made her mouth twist into a contorted frown. But even the sight of that hadn't changed the way Lloyd looked at her—which was all it took to ensure he was permanently on her mind. Especially because...

"—Hunh? Damn, the rumors are true...guess the Belt Princess actually wants to be a soldier..."

Especially because people were always cursing at her, acting like they'd had a paranormal encounter. In an instant, all her cheer drained from her face, which clamped down to radiate hostility once again.

Opening her one visible eye wide, she scanned around for the speaker—and found a muscle-bound man looming over her. He was over six feet tall and carrying a battle-ax. But despite his rough manner and appearance, he was well dressed and clearly from the upper class. One look at his figure and medals on his chest, and Selen knew who he was.

The Lidocaine family...another local lord... Known for their military honors and glory.

That was enough to make Selen decide not to poke her nose in any trouble. She turned and tromped away.

"Yo! Don't ignore me! You know how much you've damaged the reputation of the local lords?"

I'm sick of hearing about it.

She was well aware that her story was being embellished and shared around like a ghost story. And that this had caused a decline in the public opinion of all local lords.

"Shit, you're seriously creepy!" the Lidocaine man spat, making no effort to hide his irritation, and then vanished into the lights of a meal hall.

I get that a lot, Selen thought. But a few moments later, she replayed her encounter with that boy and felt herself glowing again.

When she reached the inn, Selen blew straight past the startled look of the clerk, who caught a glimpse of her blond hair springing out like ivy through the gaps in the belt, and headed straight to her room, where she removed her dirty hood and outfit and let her mind wander.

"He brushed these off for me..."

That filled her with the sudden impulse to preserve and never wash them again. But even if her face looked like this, she felt she should clean the rest of herself up, at the very least, so she filled a bucket with water and shoved her clothes in it.

Then she caught a glimpse of herself in her underwear in the mirror and was lost in thought once again.

Her pale body clad only in white underwear...thinking about all that time she'd spent pushing herself to the limits that left her figure chiseled. Like a marble statue. Her head was placed awkwardly on the top of it all, as if it'd been misplaced, wrapped in that bloodstain of a belt. In the past, looking at herself had left her feeling pained, but these days she felt nothing. Like she was looking at a stranger.

But that day was different. Her meeting with the boy, with Lloyd, had changed her. She looked at her wide-open eye and whispered, sadly, "Maybe I should try to wear some makeup."

She knew it wouldn't change anything, and that feeling clutched her heart like the belt around her head.

"If it weren't for this belt…!"

A tear formed in her eye, running down the length of the belt strap below.

The faintest of feelings she was allowing herself to explore, that future she'd started to imagine for herself…they would never come to pass, not with this constricting her.

It'd been a long while since she'd allowed herself to feel this sad. Maybe she really was in love…and that realization made the tears flow all the more.

She wept for some time. When her eyes dried, Selen glared at the belt, and then, in a flash of anger, snatched it, trying to yank it off—even if it tore her skin along with it.

A desperate impulse. Another futile attempt.

Her fingers dug in so hard they shook and her teeth ground together, as she tugged at the belt. But it remained secured on her head as hard as a rock.

Or at least, that's how it always went.

This time it slid right off.

"What?"

That was the only response Selen could manage.

She sat perfectly still for several minutes before it occurred to her to peel the rest of it off.

It didn't resist her at all, slipping right off, and she unwound the whole thing like a child unwrapping a present.

"No…way."

With the entire belt on the floor, she looked at herself in the mirror for the first time in over a decade. It was like looking at a total stranger.

The girl in the mirror had blond hair, which framed a face that could be called gorgeous. She reached up to touch it, making sure it was hers…and the beauty in the mirror did the same thing.

"Is this…me?"

The person in the mirror mouthed the same words as Selen. And then she saw tears rolling down her cheeks.

"It is…"

As Selen started to weep, she remembered the boy's face and the monk's reassurance: *Strength would free her from the curse.*

She rubbed a finger on the cheek where the boy had touched her.

"It's him," she whispered, wrapping her arms around herself. "Fate brought him to me…"

Chapter 2

A Dirty Scheme: Suppose a Wolf Had Entered a Contest Meant Only for Sheep

And just like that, it was the day of the test.

The central square below the castle in the Kingdom of Azami featured a bronze statue of the king himself. A popular tourist attraction, it welcomed throngs of people who came to look at the statue…but since his metallic figure was noticeably more fit and more handsome than the real king, the locals tended to call it the "tribute to the king's vanity."

This statue's gaze usually fell upon crowds of tourists, but today, the mood of the crowd was tense—and clearly not those of sightseers.

Just from the looks of it, everyone seemed seasoned and well trained, but they came from all sorts of backgrounds—from people decked out in expensive new outfits and equipment, to those wearing well-used breastplates, looking something like bandits, and everything in between.

Two soldiers stood in a room in the castle, looking down at the seething group from a distance. One was a male officer—he looked young, but he had the calm composure of a grizzled veteran, which was highlighted by his silver hair. The scar on his cheek drew the eye. The other was a brown-haired female officer—his opposite, as she seemed unusually hyper for her age.

Her eyes scanned the crowd eagerly, like a tourist spotting an unusual animal. If she wasn't in uniform, anyone would have taken her for a middle school student on a field trip.

"Hey-yo, Merthophan, we got us an unprecedented selection this year, eh?" she commented. She spoke with a rapid-fire accent found to the west.

Meanwhile, the male officer—Merthophan—spoke in an emotionless, flat voice, like he was reading a report aloud. "All for the peace of the realm. Skill must outweigh rank or we'll get nowhere. Am I wrong, Choline?"

The female officer—Choline—answered before he even finished. "Well, yer not wrong. I'll take a peasant who made a name for 'emselves over some spoiled rich kid any day of the—whoa!"

She'd spotted something midsentence and slapped Merthophan on the back, yelling, "Look!" as she pointed at a particularly large man.

"That's Allan Toin Lidocaine! Eldest son of a local lord; earned himself a ton of medals, I hear! He's been sweeping all the tournaments."

It appeared Allan was drawing attention not just from Choline but everyone around him. "Is that...?" Whispers rippled through the crowds, like when a celebrity was spotted in town.

But Merthophan's voice betrayed no such enthusiasm. "He's a very ambitious man. He immediately agreed to enlist on the condition that he's made an officer quickly."

"You don't say? Sounds like the noblest of noblemen. He's got the goods for sure, but I'm not feelin' it."

"Ambition stems from a strong will. As long as it's for the benefit of the realm, it isn't an issue."

Choline shook her head with extra dramatic flair at his relentless professionalism. "I know you're all riled up about this, but oy—even for peace, that one's a bit much!"

This time she was pointing at a tall, wiry woman with a mean glint in her eyes and a permanent grin on her lips. She was showing a lot of skin and sitting on the side of the road, writing in some sort of journal with an arm covered in mechanical parts—presumably an artificial limb.

Those around her were keeping their distance, which made her stand out even more. And it wasn't just the metal arm keeping people away.

"Riho Flavin...the one-armed mercenary. From the Flavin District.

Infamous for turning on employers she doesn't like—goin' on violent rampages, invading their lands, etcetera, etcetera. There's a warrant out for her arrest, ya know."

"She's a mercenary. We made a deal. Not an issue."

"What kinda deal?"

"If she enlisted, I'd get that warrant canceled."

"Well, well… I see you're in it to win it…huh?" Choline looked around the square, baffled—searching for someone she couldn't find.

"What?"

"Oh, nothin'. Just thought, all these people here, and no sign of that rumored Belt Princess."

"Are you talking about the one who spent ten years training in her bedroom to free herself from it?"

"There've been a bunch of sightings, so I wanted to get a look for myself. Eh, too bad." Choline locked her hands behind her head, muttering, "Boooooring," and turned to leave.

"Where are you going?"

"To get ready for the test. I'm in charge of the written test on magic stuff! See ya."

"You should hurry…oh, and she's already gone. Never was one to let herself be pinned down…"

Merthophan looked back down at the applicants below.

A stir ran through the crowd.

He followed their stares and found the crowd parting like the Red Sea to make way for a beautiful woman. Short blond hair, elegant features with a shadow of a brooding look that only added to her mystique. But it wasn't just her appearance that was causing this reaction.

"She's jacked," Merthophan grunted.

She might have been lightly dressed, but the curves of her chest, waist, and hips were less *bombshell* than *taut*. Her muscles honed to a catlike litheness, and she had a strange leather belt with a red stain wrapped around her waist…and when he saw that part, the pin dropped.

"Is that the Belt Princess? …Selen Hemein?"

As if echoing Merthophan's realization, a big man—Allan—called out to her. "Yo, you the Belt Princess?"

A collective murmur spread through the crowd. "Is she...?" "The rumors said..."

"......"

The woman showed no reaction to Allan's words or the stares of the crowd. This just seemed to confirm her identity.

"*Tch*...that arrogant attitude seals the deal. What the hell, man? Don't tell me that belt actually came off or that it turns out you're actually hot."

"...What's it to you?"

Her voice was clear and cold. This just wound Allan up even more.

"To hell with that!" he snarled. "You know damn well your whole creepy-ass vibe has been fueling rumors that all the local lords are deranged! If you can make yourself presentable, why didn't you do that years ago?" Allan took a big step forward, glaring down at her. "I'd have been promoted way faster without you around."

Watching this conflict from a distance, Merthophan put his hand to his chin, as he thought, *He's got the skills but seems a little to rash... Well, it's not so bad that we can't train it out of him.*

But even as he calmly considered the man's future potential...

"—Pffft!" Stone-faced, Merthophan suddenly shot out snot, achieving a record distance. "—Hot damn!" he yelped, rattled enough to break character. He'd just seen—

"Anywhere to sit down?" called out a boy in a simple linen shirt, looking around him as he walked.

But this was no ordinary boy. His sheer strength radiated off every step...toughness beyond all measure, power that you'd never imagine from his appearance.

"That boy's applying?" Merthophan gulped, oblivious to the snot dribbling down his chin. "Good lord...with him as a patriotic soldier, our military force will be without rival in a decade or two. Even if war broke out today, we'd never lose!"

Merthophan thanked the gods for bringing this boy to him. Snot was still trickling down his chin.

Meanwhile, the infamous mercenary Riho was sitting at the edge of the square, watching Allan and Selen going at it with a grin.

"Got some spicy ones here," she muttered as she evaluated their strength.

Ax dude's strong enough, but in a tournament pro kinda way. He's good one-on-one, but not so much in a real war... While Belt Princess's definitely put in the hours, but she's got no experience in actual combat.

She scribbled this down in her notebook.

Both are from big-shot families in the central region...which means they're filthy rich.

Riho Flavin was appraising everyone here based primarily on potential cash flows; her notes were filled with details on how she could use them for her financial gain. To a mercenary, the secret to success was finding clients she could control and work with; she'd learned the hard way through one brush with death after another.

She finished scribbling down her evaluations, snapped her notebook closed, and put it away, before taking a deep breath.

All right. She wiped the sweat from her hands on her trousers. *Time to face reality.*

With that ominous thought, Riho slowly turned her gaze to her side.

"Whew...finally found an open space to sit down!"

Who is this freak of nature?!

Next to Riho, a boy with a cheery expression plopped down, wearing a simple linen shirt that made it abundantly clear he didn't have any money. At a glance, there was nothing extraordinary about him...

You can't tell by looking, but this is no ordinary boy! Just sitting next to him has the hairs on my back rising!

She'd never experienced anything like this. She'd often run into

©Nao Watanuki

people who made her want to book it, but this was the first time she'd ever felt like she wouldn't be able to outrun her opponent.

I…I can't even move…it feels like if I moved a muscle or let my guard down, it'd give him the chance to send my head flying… It's like I'm looking death in the face!

It felt like a tiger had just sat down next to her. Like one false move would attract his attention—with dire consequences.

Crap…crap! …Definitely underestimated this place…I never thought anyone like him would try to join the damn army!

Sweat pouring down her face, she kept her breathing shallow, trying to remain undetected, but…

"Um, can I ask you something?"

The tiger—Lloyd—turned and looked right at her.

"Eep!"

With a squeak, Riho threw her left arm up in front of herself defensively.

"…That's amazing. A mechanical arm?"

Oh shit, I've made a mistake, Riho thought. Raising her craggy arm could be taken as a sign of aggression.

Crap! I gotta choose my next words carefully—ack, my life depends on it!

She swiftly lowered the arm, smiling awkwardly.

A
Riho: "Oh, yes! It's a mechanical arm."
Lloyd: "Then it must feel no pain!" *Riiiippp*

B
Riho: "No, I was born with it."
Lloyd: "Liar!" *Riiiippp*

C
Riho: "……" Silence.
Lloyd: "Say something!" *Riiiippp*

* * *

Every scenario in her mind ended with her mechanical arm being torn off, and visions of her future flashed before her eyes.

My life…is over…

Seeing the look on her face, Lloyd spluttered, "Oh, sorry, didn't mean to pry. I just thought it looked really cool!"

The smile he gave her was certainly gentle. Even comforting. *Is that how the devil smiles?* she thought, even more on edge than before.

Oblivious to the inner workings of her mind, Lloyd kept chattering away. "I'm from way out in the countryside, you see. I don't really know anyone here, so I was feeling pretty nervous and uh…oh, I'm Lloyd, by the way. Lloyd Belladonna."

"Er, uh…Riho. Flavin."

Certain she'd die if she didn't accept his handshake, she put both hands around it like a campaigning politician, bowing her head low. Her weight shifted so she could leap backward at a moment's notice.

The awkward tension between them was broken by the sudden intrusion of the Belt Princess, Selen.

Wh-what now?! The friggin' Belt Princess?!

Selen had been scanning the crowd, assuming that anyone who could beat that locust monster would either be a soldier already or here to enlist. This hunch had paid off, and fate had brought them together again. The thought of it made a broad smile spread across her faintly flushed face. Until now, the belt around her face had made an awful creaking noise every time she smiled, but she no longer had to hear that awful cacophony.

Riho knew none of this and braced herself to handle this new arrival.

This new girl had on a euphoric expression, looking like she'd never been happier in her entire life. She came right over to Lloyd and clicked her heels together, ready to say something—but she'd clearly failed to think of a topic beforehand.

"Oh, Sir Lloyd, Sir Lloyd, Sir Lloyd…"

Erm, well, it might be a bigger problem than finding common ground. The language centers of her brain appeared to be on the fritz.

As she stood there muttering to herself, Lloyd looked briefly confused, but she seemed familiar, and she was the right height. From those scant clues, he was able to conclude that this must be the skewer girl.

"Oh, Selen, was it?" he asked, all smiles. "You're here to enlist, too?"

"Yes! I'm Selen Hemein, and I'm all yours!"

Onlookers could almost see the question mark forming above Lloyd's head at the last line— far more suitable for pillow talk than the current situation. But he decided it was best to ignore it.

Is this my chance to escape? Riho was certainly curious about whatever was going on between these two but figured it was best to leave while she could. She dropped down on all fours to make her exit.

"And? Who are you?" Selen asked, the light leaving her eyes as she turned toward Riho at the worst possible time. Her gaze featured the dull gleam of a girl who'd spotted a rival for her love's affections.

"—Dammit! Ugh!" With her one chance to leave crushed, Riho glared up at Selen without righting herself.

"Seemed like you and Lloyd were getting cozy with each other?"

"Cozy?! Are you friggin' blind?!" Riho looked into those dead eyes, whispering, "Oh shit, you're actually blind," just as Lloyd jumped in, trying to drown out her last comment.

"This is Riho. We only just met a second ago."

This cheered Selen up considerably.

"You did? Your interaction seemed strange, so I thought you might be a rival for his love…"

How did abject terror register as that?! Wait…

Riho had an idea, looking like a light bulb was going off above her.

A local lord and a country boy… They shouldn't be connected in any way, but they seem awfully close. They must have history.

From her perspective…it seemed that they were certainly close, if they weren't an item already, though it did seem like one was more into the other. She would have been genuinely shocked to discover they were basically total strangers.

I can sense power from this Lloyd person, enough to raise my hackles…

but maybe I can work an angle through his connection to the Belt Princess and make use of him.

In Riho's mind, she was a ringmaster ordering a lion tamer (Selen) to make the ferocious Lloyd do her bidding. Her old grin came back.

If I can get her to control this monster for me, I can move mountains… and make bank even when I'm stuck in this dismal army. I can almost taste that money!

This was a radical change in perspective—from fear for her life to a shot at a big score. Riho was already pumping her fist at the idea.

Meanwhile, the savage beast, Lloyd, was still smiling very gently.

"Well, glad to make some friends…I mean, first I've got to pass this test…"

On the other hand, the target of Riho's would-be manipulations— Selen—was beaming and muttering to herself.

"Sir Lloyd" times twenty. *Mumble, mumble.*

…………And as each dwelled on their own thoughts, the admissions test was about to begin.

Under a clear blue sky, the crowd had been divided into a number of groups to administer the test. Colonel Merthophan had been putting a lot of work into recruiting in recent years, and the staff was used to guiding throngs of people by now, so things flowed smoothly. Hearty voices calling out "Next!" echoed across the square. First up was the combat test.

"Right, use any weapon of your choice and attack the dummy. We'll take a look at your agility and fighting style… And we don't care if you chop the thing in half!"

This last line got a big laugh out of the crowd. The dummy was made of stacks and stacks of iron plates, while the weapons were cheap bronze; there was no way these things could ever cut the dummies in half. Normally.

But Lloyd's standards for everything—humor included—were totally out of whack. "But it looks like it'll be easy to cut in half," he said to himself, cocking his head to the side, and remained unsure why everyone else was laughing.

While Lloyd was waiting his turn, Merthophan was watching the test from a distance, nodding with a look of great satisfaction.

"It was worth the effort to gather them here... If these people are willing to fight for their country, we'll be ready for any surprise."

Riho saw him standing with his arms folded and left her place in line, flexing her powerful-looking false arm. She trotted over to him, grinning.

"............What? Not going to drop out now, are you?" the officer commented.

"Heh, don't make me laugh. You're paying me on top of flushing all my sins away... I'll put up with a lot for that. Not about to let a deal this good get away."

"Then what do you want?" he asked, suspicious.

"Oh, you know," she started, continuing to be super chill. "You're sure putting a lot of work into this test. You got me, the Belt Princess—lots of people here with interesting stories to 'em."

"All for the future of the realm."

"Yeah, yeah. Anyway...my question is..." She jabbed a finger in Lloyd's direction. "The frick is that?"

"—No friggin' clue."

This uncharacteristic response made Riho lean in. "Like hell! You scouted him, right? That one's wild!"

"I'm as shocked as you! We could have everyone here, myself included, gang up on him, and I don't know if we'd win..."

Riho saw how nervous Lloyd looked and shook her head.

"He looks like any other country boy, but...that makes him even more frightening. I was legit worried my instincts were all messed up or something."

Something about her tone must have reminded Merthophan of his position, because his tone grew immediately professional again. "I know you're curious, but during the trial, I must remain impartial.

Return to your place. If you get yourself disqualified, you'll just be another criminal."

"Yeah, yeah, whatever. Guess we'll find out how strong he really is after I pass this thing."

"You seem confident. You sure you're up to it?"

"You're the one who scouted me, Colonel."

She flashed him a grin. Behind her, the test administrator called her name.

She waved her artificial hand, heading over to the proctor.

"—What weapon will you use, Riho Flavin?"

Sword, mace, ax…she glanced over the array of weapons jammed in the wooden box as she continued to smile.

"Something funny?"

"Nothing, just…you're asking me that?" She whipped her left arm out in front of the administrator.

The machinery inside started to whir like a long-horned beetle, leaving him speechless. She took a quick leap over to the dummy, swinging her arm toward it. There was a screech of metal on metal, and the dummy's iron plate came off, landing on the ground with a sharp clang.

"That…that was welded on!"

Riho just grinned at him. "My buddy here's made of mithril, so this is nothing. You pass me, and I'm sure it can be a big help to Azami. Just between you and me, though, this thing is useful but costs an arm and a leg to maintain. So help a girl out, would ya?"

"…Bring a new dummy!"

With her sales pitch over, Riho headed toward the next test area.

"So come on, Lloyd, m'lady Selen…I need you both to pass this thing."

Meanwhile, in front of Lloyd in line, the decorated veteran Allan Lidocaine was about to show off his strength.

"Hrgh, hyah, rah, hah! Argh!"

As he swung a heavy two-handed ax around like it weighed nothing, Allan hacked at the dummy from all directions. The crowd watching *ooh*ed and *aah*ed, sounding very impressed.

"That's enough! Next!"

"Hmph, good workout."

When Allan was done, Lloyd thought, *Oh, I see. This isn't about knocking the dummy down; it's a test to see if we can hit it on beat—and fast! So that's how people are scored!*

Convinced he was being scored on artistic merit like a figure skater, Lloyd grew even more nervous. "This is gonna be hard...," he whispered, cowering slightly.

"Next! Lloyd Belladonna!"

"Uh, here!"

His voice cracked in the middle, and it got a snicker from the crowd around him, but he was too tense to notice. He was stressing so hard his right and left leg both moved together as a pair.

"Ahem. Your weapon?"

"Er, uh, ah, a short sword."

Lloyd rummaged around to draw a little sword from the box and hastily readied himself. When he gingerly approached the dummy, the crowd sneered.

Gently, gently...don't break it...but multiple attacks, rhythmically...

Approaching it as if the slightest touch would break it, Lloyd swung his blade too fast for the eye to see.

Literally too fast for the eye to see—the other people in line and the test administrator had no idea what happened.

But a few seconds later...the dummy fell to pieces—with a heavy crash and a huge puff of dust.

""""Hunh?!"""" The crowd gaped.

Lloyd misinterpreted the crowd's disbelief as horror at his failure (like, "come on, seriously?") and hung his head.

Ohhhhh nooooooooooooooo...

The administrator looked back and forth at the dejected boy and the broken dummy. "Hmm...I guess Allan's attacks had made it kinda fragile...like it was already broken *before you even touched it.*"

Yeah, that must be it.

"Enough! Hey! Bring another dummy, quick!" he shouted, trying to move Lloyd along.

Lloyd dragged his feet as he left, desperately thinking about how he could make up for this on the written test.

Next up was the written component. The administrators were already gathering the completed test sheets.

"Hmm? What the...?"

One administrator's eyes happened to fall on a test sheet with a very strange answer.

"Lloyd Belladonna...what the hell is this answer?"

The question involved was a simple one: *List some examples of fire magic.* But the answer was a list of unreadable pictographs.

"Oh, I see. Your classic 'I-don't-get-it-so-I'll-just-make-something-up' answer, huh? Happens all in the time in vocab quizzes, ha-ha-ha."

He finished gathering the tests, certain that anyone dumb enough to have to fudge this question with drawings was definitely doomed.

Neither the administrator nor the people grading the tests knew that these pictographs were runes, wisdom of yore.

While the test papers were being collected, the applicant interviews were going on in the next room. Lloyd was facing two administrators, sweating like he was in a sauna.

"Lloyd Belladonna, was it?"

"Yes, I came here hoping to be a soldier..."

"From Kunlun...never heard of it. Where is it?"

"Oh, uh, the very edge of the continent."

"What edge...? Whatever. Any special skills we should know about?"

"Er, uh...cooking, laundry, and, um...I can make it rain."

This last one earned him a look of surprise.

"—Hunh?"

"Th-that's about it. Um..."

Lloyd stood up, went to the window, scribbled something on the wooden frame, and made a gesture like he was shooing it toward the sky. He'd cast a rain spell using an ancient rune, but to the administrators, it looked like total mumbo jumbo. They glanced at each other and winced.

"...All right. So, uh, in a few minutes it should start raining."

"That's enough. Exit's that way."

"Oh… Okay."

Lloyd's shoulders slumped forward, and he trailed out of the room.

"—No hope for him," one administrator commented.

The other one nodded. "Rain? Mm? Wait…is it clouding over…?"

He frowned. "Must be some cheap farmer trick. Read the flow of the clouds or whatever, then pretend like you're making it rain."

"Like that'd fool us."

"Exactly. If anyone could do that, it would be a huge deal."

Together, they looked at the raindrops striking the window and left it at that.

Once the test concluded, Lloyd's shoulders were still drooped as he trudged home.

"Ah…I knew making it rain wasn't a big deal…"

He was getting soaked as he weaved through the streets. He was too filled with self-loathing to even bother avoiding the puddles.

When will he ever realize just how powerful he really is?

And on the day the results were posted, a middle-aged neighbor came to visit Marie's shop, where Lloyd was staying. She had tendinitis or something, which made her elbow ache, and kept rubbing the place she'd applied a minty ointment.

As Marie ground up a new batch of herbs for her, the woman was chattering away from behind.

"That's the long and short of it, Marie. The king's in bad shape and almost never leaves his room anymore."

"Is that true?"

"Oh, absolutely! My daughter works in the palace, and she says so, which means it must be true. And listen to this: Rumor has it all the bigwigs are in a panic. Like war could break out at any second."

"I've been hearing that a lot. I'm not so sure, though, 'cause there must be a lot of people arguing against it."

"Certainly, certainly. That's why there's been a lot of back-and-forth about whether to start getting the troops ready. And lately, the roads in the city have been exploding, and the river got clogged up—you know, the one the merchants use. All that was bolstering talk of war, but suddenly, all those problems just went away so the anti-war folks have been able to push back."

"Oh, right…*I wonder why…*," Marie said, unable to admit the solution to these problems had been her freeloading guest, and busied herself with her tea.

"The merchants are calming down, too, saying, 'Was that really the work of the Jiou Empire? Or were our leaders just trying to distract us from how unprepared they were to deal with crisis?' They say the king really wants a war, so the opposition wants to get the princess on their side—but she's missing; and they're looking everywhere for her; and maybe the whole fight over the war is why she went missing in the first...owww..."

"See? You get yourself all worked up, and... Here you go, it's ready."

The old hag grasped her elbow as if it were punishing her for her rapid-fire, tongue-splitting gossip. Marie seized her chance to proffer the finished ointment.

"Oh, thanks so much. You're sure you don't need anything?"

"Don't worry about it! You let me hear all the latest buzz from the castle, right?"

"Well...the next time we've got leftovers, I'm bringing you some."

"Sounds good."

The neighbor took the bottle with a smile and started to leave.

"...Oh, I've been meaning to ask, Marie," she added, turning back at the door. Her smile had broadened—into a gleeful grin, ready to dish the dirt. "Is that new boy your you-know-what?"

Bam! Rattle! Crash!

"Where'd *that* come from?!" Marie gasped, so startled by this surprise attack that she'd hurled her mortar into the kitchen.

"Well, you used to always get sick of eating canned food and come around to beg for a home-cooked meal, but lately, you haven't shown up at all, so all the housewives have been starting to wonder...and then one eyewitness after another stepped forward..."

"H-he isn't! He's a relative's...oh, right! I'm a witch! It shouldn't be weird for me to have an apprentice! I make him do my cooking!"

"Oh, well, I didn't realize witches these days tenderly fix their apprentice's bedheads or wave at them when they depart until they're out of sight?"

Marie clearly remembered doing both of those things and turned so red it looked like steam was about to pour out of her ears.

"Just how much did you see?! And how did you know that?"

"Oh, she's gone all scary. Time to beat a hasty retreat!" The woman turned and dashed out of the shop.

She was probably running off to gossip about this conversation with the other neighborhood biddies. Marie pictured her blunder being regurgitated like food for a nest of hatchlings and turned bright red again.

Marie was all too aware of these instances, which made it impossible to make excuses. She'd been unable to stop herself fussing over the boy, and by now, she definitely knew what that young hag saw in the kid. Her own hypocrisy left her awkwardly scratching her cheek.

"Urgh…maybe some coffee will calm me down…"

She abandoned the idea of cleaning up after her work and went to make a fresh brew. As the scent of it filled the air, she slowly regained control over her emotions.

And her mind was finally able to start processing the news from the castle.

War at any second, huh? That rockslide, the clogged-up river, the monsters appearing…seems like those are all connected. All trying to push us into a battle.

She took a sip of her coffee, grimacing.

"—If I had it together, none of this would be happening…"

"Howdy, dumbo Marie! Gimme some coffee, too!"

Her pigtailed elder *loli* master had just walked out of the closet like she owned the place.

Marie glared at Alka, yelling, "And then I wouldn't have needed you breathing down my neck! What is it this time?!"

She angrily shoved a cup of coffee at her master. Alka perched on a chair, doing her best to cross her wittle feetsies, and answered as if nothing was out of the ordinary.

"Huh? Ain't the test results out today? He'll pass; there'll be a celebration; and I'm fixin' to steal a smooch in the joy of the moment."

"Damn you, ten-year-old Marie! Why did you ever think it was a good idea to let this little shit in your life?!"

Marie clutched her head, and Alka added more sugar…and a little bit more sugar to her coffee.

"Well, even if he somehow fails…if you regain your authority, you can fix that."

Alka flashed Marie a meaningful look, the edges of her lips curling up in a devious grin.

"After all, you're the missing princess of Azami…Princess Maria."

Marie's pose as she clawed at her own head reached avant-garde levels. No one who saw her like this would ever believe she was the princess. They'd just turn around and request an eye exam and a brain scan.

"Is that why you sent Lloyd to me?!"

"Right on…he's a good boy, so I figured you'd grow fond of him. But…I reckon you might be a little *too* fond of him. I'd better do something before you start foreshadowing something to come in your future…"

Alka's gaze had latched onto Marie's brooch…and Marie shuddered.

At this rate, she really would start to presage something—her death. This fear got her tongue working.

"Oh, I dunno about *fond*! He's like a brother! Uh, and it's gonna be a while before I go back to the whole princess thing—can't do that until I find out who's behind this whole war thing."

"Yeah, yeah. Whatever. Let's focus on Lloyd. How's my boy?"

Alka had always been dismissive of things that actually mattered. Even as Marie inwardly shook her head, she did her best to answer.

"Uh, he came back from the test looking real dejected. And…"

"Well, that boy's never had a high opinion of himself. And what? Somethin' else going on with him?"

"Not directly with him. But there's a beautiful girl going around asking questions, trying to find him."

"Oh?"

"Saying destiny brought them together."

"…………Oh."

The temperature in the shop seemed to drop.

"Um, Master?"

"……………Maybe Lloyd wasn't dejected because of the test. Maybe it was *lovesickness*."

"*Masteeer!*"

"That's it! I'll have to destroy this country!"

"You idiot! You can't just go straight to annihilation every time something inconveniences you! Remember that time you tried to destroy the country because the number of strawberries on your parfait didn't match the picture on the menu?!"

"Ohhhh, why did you remind me?! Now I have to level the country TWICE!"

"Once is plenty! No, once is bad enough! Get it together, *loli* Grandma!"

The people of Azami were better off not knowing how many times the land had nearly perished and how many times Marie had managed to save them.

Riho Flavin had a fearsome reputation.

She was infamous enough that you only had to say *one-armed mercenary* and everyone would know you meant her. From the barely-better-than-underwear clothing covering her svelte frame, to the piercing almond eyes that didn't even bother hiding her rotten personality, to the mechanical arm far too bulky for her size—all of it served to draw the eye and tell you to keep your distance.

With her arm as her partner, she'd done whatever it took to keep the money rolling in. Her prickly attitude, single-minded fixation on cash, and impulsive streak led to an endless string of trouble. She'd done everything from refusing to pay tolls to turning on and injuring unsavory clients, and these troubles had mounted until she became a wanted criminal.

The officers baited her into becoming a student at the military school by promising to pardon these crimes. Naturally, she had no plans to stop there; she was hell-bent on using her fellow students and superiors to earn herself some serious cash flow.

The day of the admissions results, a huge crowd of applicants gathered around big boards outside the gates, scanning the posted papers for their application number. If it was there, it meant they got in. Otherwise, they were shit outta luck.

Riho found her own number on the list—not that there was any doubt—and, ignoring the frightened looks around her, stomped over to the lecture room where the admitted students were seated. She found herself an empty desk and kicked back to observe the crowd.

Most of my targets are here… Good, good.

The observations in her notebook wouldn't go to waste.

Then her eyes lit upon Selen. Was the Belt Princess uncomfortable? She seemed to be looking for something.

Oh…probably that boy she's in love with.

Riho was pretty sure she was looking for Lloyd.

That boy…she'd never met anyone without a limit to their strength. All the life-threatening situations she'd been through, and he still managed to spook her. But he looked so much like any old country boy, and his smile had been so open and friendly that she'd genuinely been unsure if her instincts were leading her awry.

Riho had him down as a key player in her plans to turn this school thing into a gravy train.

If Lloyd's here, challenging quests and dangerous business will be easy… if I can ride his coattails, I'll make bank…hmm?

She discovered the problem. Lloyd wasn't here. Riho's head was soon scanning the room as much as Selen's.

"You've gotta be kidding me…"

As Riho reeled in disbelief, she felt someone behind her. She spun around to find…

"What, you're tellin' me the one-armed mercenary passed?"

The eldest Lidocaine boy, Allan.

"—Not now," Riho said curtly and started looking through the crowd again.

Summarily dismissed, Allan elected not to try again. He beat a hasty retreat, and to cheer himself up, he decided to take a jab at Selen.

"Yo, Belt…"

"—Not now."

After he'd been shooed away twice in a row, Allan went and sat in a corner, tears welling up in his eyes. He spent a while muttering, "Why *not* now?" at his desk.

After some time, two figures appeared at the podium—Merthophan, with his stone face, and Choline, who looked like she was enjoying herself thoroughly.

"Everyone's here?" called out a voice with gravitas and authority, which instantly silenced the crowd. He nodded approvingly.

But a few moments later, Merthophan's calm facade faded, and he started surveying the students, just like Riho and Selen. His expression remained resolute, but his behavior grew increasingly odd; he turned his head like a revolving fan, looking around and around the room without a word.

"Er? What's up, Merthophan?"

He grabbed the list of names, looking it over, muttering, "Impossible," under his breath. "This can't be," he whimpered, like he'd failed the test himself.

"Merthophan…we need to get start…"

"Uh…anyone late? Anyone in the bathroom? Are we abso-friggin'-lutely sure this is everyone?!"

"Um, Merthophan? You're breaking character…"

"Right! Raise your hand if you're *not* here!"

"Merthophan! Dignity! Authority!" Choline squeaked, unable to watch her colleague reduce himself to a goofball punch line. She clearly decided it was best if she took over. "*Ahem.* Congrats on passing, people!"

But she was immediately interrupted. Someone from the crowd had stepped forward, hand raised, asking a question.

"Um, excuse me? There should be someone named Lloyd here…or did he not pass?"

It was Selen. She looked downright beside herself.

Yeesh, Choline thought and tried to talk sense into her. "Now, now, Belt Princess. You ask a personal question like that here, no tellin' how Merthophan might decide to punish ya."

Merthophan was all about regulations, impartiality, and order. Choline was genuinely concerned for this girl. But…

"I thought the same thing!" Merthophan roared. "There must be some mistake!"

"You're with her, granite-face?!"

Seeing Merthophan acting this way gave her an all-new reason for concern. Was he broken, somehow? He tossed the registry to Choline and began to leave the room.

"Choline, take over! I'm gonna go interrogate the administrators!"

"Huh?!"

While Choline gaped after him, Selen tried to follow.

"I'll join you!"

"Whoa, you're a student now! You can't skip out on orientation!"

If she did, Merthophan would…but before she could finish the thought…

"Yeah! Come with me!" he bellowed with a thumbs-up, as if welcoming a like-minded soul. Choline gave him a look like she had no idea who he was.

"Mind if I join you?" Riho asked, joining the fray. A good chance to get closer to Selen and learn a little more about Lloyd. Her motivations were clearly suspicious, yet…

"Yes, do. Glad to have you on board," Merthophan said, as if welcoming reinforcements. His expression remained stony, but he now had *both* thumbs raised, his entire body emanating warmth.

Even Riho winced a little.

Was he always like this? Eh, whatever.

The three of them quickly strode out of the room, ditching Choline, who stood there with her jaw open.

*   *   *

Team Lloyd was headed to the interview site, of course. A colonel, a gorgeous student, and a female mercenary were a ragtag group you'd never expect to see together, and they turned eyes wherever they went.

Merthophan pulled the test data, found the lead interviewer's name, and summoned him at once.

"Grab his legs, Riho."

"Roger that."

"Er, are you…Colonel Merthophan! What are you…?"

"Save your excuses."

"Hunhhh? What's going oooon?!"

…Please excuse this error: It was more like they kidnapped him and moved him bodily into the nearest empty lecture hall. There, Merthophan expressionlessly slammed his hand into the wall next to the forty-something male administrator like something out of a tawdry romance manga. Not that anyone asked for such a scene.

"I understand you interviewed Lloyd Belladonna."

The interviewer was flanked by the Belt Princess and the one-armed mercenary…guaranteeing death in all directions. He went pale and nodded vigorously.

"Good…then I'll get right to the point… Why did you fail him?"

"Well, you see, he just started babbling nonsense at the interview!"

"Professing his love for me?!"

"Shut it, Belt Princess."

"Oh, sorry, right, that wouldn't be considered nonsense at all, since we're in l-o-v-e… I'm sorry, who are you again?"

"Oh, don't do me dirty like that, m'lady Selen! We're gonna get along great," chirped Riho.

Ignoring the comedy set on either side of him, Merthophan pressed the interviewer further, his eyes glinting like steel. "What kind of nonsense?"

"Like…we asked what he was good at. And he said he could make it rain!"

"…………Rain?"

Team Lloyd frowned as one. The interviewer seemed to calm down a little, color returning to his face. He adjusted his collar.

"Yup. That's exactly how I reacted, sir."

"But it did actually rain. I remember it raining," Selen commented.

"Well, country folk often know how to read the skies and predict how the weather will change. But doing that and then lying about making it rain yourself? We're not that stupid."

The interviewer was now so confident he was boasting about his professional excellence. This left Merthophan without a leg to stand on.

"If anyone could really do that, we'd never have to worry about losing crops to drought...but he might... Really, though? Rain? That's..."

That was too much to believe. Merthophan leaned against the wall, and the interviewer slammed his hand against it next to the colonel's head. Their positions reversed. (Again, no one really asked for this kind of fan service.)

"And on top of that, he scribbled a bunch of doodles in the answer field for a basic question on his magic test... The army doesn't need someone like that."

"Doodles? He didn't seem the type," Riho chimed in. Lloyd had struck her as extremely diligent. The other two seemed of the same mind.

"Can we get a look at that answer sheet? I'd like to confirm this with my own eyes."

"...You're sure about that, Colonel Merthophan?"

"Sorry for the trouble. But this just doesn't add up."

"This is very unlike you...but very well. Give me a minute."

Looking a little disgruntled, the man left the room and came back with an answer sheet. He spread it out on the table, and Team Lloyd gathered around like they were gazing at a treasure map.

The multiple-choice answers were all marked correct...but below them, the essay question was filled with rows of unreadable symbols... more pictures than letters. These were obviously...

"Doodles."

"Definitely doodles."

"Yup, just doodles."

Doodles they were.

"Well…this is…I don't know what to say."

Team Lloyd groaned like a layman gazing upon contemporary art. Then a shrill voice echoed across the room.

"Hey! Merthophan! Whaddaya think you're doing?!"

Choline came into the room waving the roster around. She came running over to them and slapped Merthophan with the roll of papers right in the butt.

"*Hngg!* C-Choline! Thanks for your help."

"Have ya cooled off a bit now? Or do I need to use an ice spell on you? Oy! I had to do the whole thing myself! …Don't yell at me if I forgot anything. And you know how much harm you did to your 'stickler for regulations' rep? Geez! You definitely owe me a parfait on our next day off!"

"Uh…sorry…"

Choline's words fired out like a machine gun until Merthophan finally apologized.

She sighed deeply, shaking her head at him. "…And? What's with this Lloyd dude? You three idiots satisfied yet?"

Selen held out the answer sheet. "He's such a creative soul that the answer sheet couldn't contain him! And he even demonstrated his sense of humor in the interview! The army absolutely needs him. You should pass him immediately and make him my roommate, stat!"

"I'm sorry. This is the military academy. I think you've got it confused with the school for aspiring comedians."

"Colonel Choline, take back your insults. She's the only idiot here." Riho rubbed her temples.

"Honestly, the interviewer made the right call," Merthophan said, his voice level. "I believe he would have been an asset, but we'll have to find some other way for him to join our ranks."

"—Hang on."

"…I know. I don't usually fixate on any one individual like this, but I sensed enormous potential from him. As did Riho…"

"—Shuddup, shuddup! You, Belt Princess! Gimme that answer sheet!" Choline snatched the paper from her hands, cutting Merthophan off.

"Wh-what is it, Choline?" Merthophan asked. "Not often you look so serious."

She ignored him, her eyes boring into the sheet.

"These…are ancient runes!"

""""Ancient runes?"""" they chorused.

"Yup, they were lost long ago, and our research staff are working to crack 'em. I've never seen these ones in particular, but there's enough in common with the ones I know…definitely checks out."

"Hmm. So that's what ancient runes look like…," Merthophan commented.

Choline turned toward him, eyes bugging out of her head. "—*You* said we should research 'em! *You* said it was for the good of the realm! And now you act like you know nothing about them?! You know, I *thought* you never thanked me for all my hard work!"

"S-sorry…they're just so different from any runes I know."

Riho stepped in before they could start to fight for real. "Now, now…so what exactly are ancient runes?"

"Well, well, well. Are you interested?" Choline asked with the finesse of a seasoned sales assistant.

She quickly sent the interviewer packing and sat the three of them down in the lecture hall chairs as she launched into a full-blown speech.

"Ancient runes are believed to be a form of magic used in the ancient civilization—only traces of which remain. Where magic is normally done through incantations and using staves or jewels as an intermediary…"

"Sorry, can you get to the point?" Riho yawned, sounding bored already.

Choline coughed once. "They're super-old, really powerful magic," she concluded.

"Ta."

"...I think that might be a bit *too* simplified," Merthophan interjected.

"Gimme a sec. I'll show you how insane they are. Take this answer sheet..."

Choline began cutting out the runes one at a time.

"Basically, you can cast all kinds of spells with them by shuffling these words together. Yep, that's the gist of it. This question is asking for a fireball spell, so I'm assuming the three runes here are *fire*, *ball*, and *discharge*. Er, probably...I only know *discharge*, so this is all a guess. Just playin' it by ear."

"Probably? A guess? Sounds like you're blindly groping through this," Riho muttered.

"Good point!" Choline said with a big grin. Riho was starting to find her annoying, but she did her best not to show it. Choline was a superior officer, after all.

"You see, playing it by ear is a big part of it! With ancient runes, you can't just scribble a bunch of 'em down. You've got to keep the feel of the spell in mind when you write them. Take a look at this one. Looks like the symbol itself is going to catch on fire, doesn't it?"

"...I see, and that's why they were confused for doodles," Selen said.

"That explains why I didn't recognize them," Merthophan nodded.

"You know how the covers of comics and novels use fonts that match the tone of the book?" Choline asked. "Same thing. Knowing the right runes isn't enough. You gotta be able to instill the right feeling in 'em—and a dash of magic power."

"But if you know the runes and can draw them with the right feel, you can do basically anything."

"In theory. I mean, if ya wrote the runes for *world*, *destroy*, *dragon*, and *summon*, with the feel of summoning a world-destroying dragon..."

A world-destroying dragon? Now that's an extreme example. It made all three of them gulp nervously.

"Aaaaand you put enough magic power into it to destroy the world, you could totally summon one."

"If you have enough magic power to do that, would you even need the runes?" Riho countered, as if demanding a refund for her swallowed spit.

"Well, it's just an example! If anyone like that really existed, the world woulda been destroyed ages ago!"

Meanwhile, at the Witch of the East Side's home...

"That's it, I'm destroying the world! Who needs a world where Lloyd isn't mine!"

"Stoppp! Don't use runes for that! You're being rash! I promise you're letting your imagination get the best of you!"

Marie was busy saving the world again.

"Anyway, the main takeaway: Ancient runes are incredible things. You can do way more stuff than with our current spells—assuming the right vocabulary, technique, and raw magic power. They ain't real efficient in that regard."

"Can you use them, Colonel Choline?"

She grimaced. "Well...I kinda can, but it takes ages, and the success rate ain't great... Chanting is way easier. Like, we found ancient runes that can make a meteor fall, but nobody has enough magic to pull that off...so all the research we've done to bring them back hasn't reaped much."

Choline hung her head. Riho asked the obvious question.

"What's the point of bringing something back if you can't use it?"

"Well, we did have a candidate. Someone with top-class magic power," Merthophan answered. His tone somewhat grim. "The missing princess—Maria Azami."

Meanwhile, at the Witch of the East Side's home...

"Achooo!"

"Ughhh! My eyes! Royal germs in my eyes!"

"What the heck are royal germs?! I mean, sorry! I'm sure someone must be gossiping about me! It wasn't intention—"

"Right, I've got to disinfect the entire world now!"

"Doooooooon't!"

The threat to the world kept growing greater.

"Maria's capacity for magic was beyond the bounds of most humans. More than enough to handle ancient runes. That's why we were studying the meteor one—for the coming war, as a final resort against the Jiou Empire. But when she vanished, the plans stalled… Where could she be?"

Merthophan stared at the sky outside the window. He had no way of knowing that she was running a shop nearby in the East Side, battling fiercely to protect the fate of the world.

"I had my doubts about whether she'd agree to learn a spell that nasty—war or no war."

"For the sake of the realm, I'm sure she'd agree…no, we'd make her agree." Merthophan's final words were little more than a whisper, and no one present heard them.

Choline clapped her hands together as if just remembering something.

"Oh, right! The princess thing reminds me. I already told all the other army candidates."

"Ah…*that*." A cloud passed over Merthophan's face.

Riho didn't let it pass. "Hmm? Colonel Merthophan, dude, you're frowning."

"Right-o, I'd better bring you two up to speed. Look here."

Choline held out a piece of a straw paper and a photograph.

The former had some stiff letters punched on it with a typewriter, and the latter showed a mega-pure-looking ten-year-old girl smiling in an expensive-looking chair.

Riho narrowed her eyes, running them over the written section. When she finished reading, she sounded surprised. "…A search order for the missing princess?"

"Yeah, the girl in the photo is the missing princess, Maria Azami. It's five years out of date, though."

"I could tell she was a big shot, but…the bigger question is why such a major deal is being sent round to rookies?"

Merthophan answered. "The army has been searching for her for quite some time with no results. Our superiors are vainly hoping to solve the problem with a numbers game."

He was clearly not on board with this plan.

"And you don't approve, Colonel?" Selen asked.

"Yeah, with the foundation-day festival approaching, we need to whip the recruits into shape as soon as possible...and year after year, we get idiots after the reward making trouble, and I've got to clean up after their shit."

Riho's eyes started gleaming at the mention of a reward. She read that part out loud, excited. "Not just the money! A promotion, and they'll agree to any requests within reason...damn, that's quite a reward."

She whistled aloud.

Choline puffed herself up. "Ain't it?"

The stone-faced man next to her shot her a glare, clearly unsure why she was taking credit.

Choline ignored him, explaining, "See, the search is going nowhere fast. They figured dangling a carrot over some enthusiastic new recruits couldn't hurt. If we can get the princess to safety before anything bad happens, totally worth it."

"I hear activity among Jiou agents is picking up, too... That explains the reward," Riho commented, with a satisfied grin. Her mental abacus was adding this bonus to what she stood to gain from getting Lloyd enlisted.

"The other recruits are all fired up! That one dude more than anyone... Allan, was it?"

"It's not going to make a difference—doesn't matter how many officer cadets we throw at it. Rather than waste their time, we should be making them lift weights. Selen Hemein, Riho Flavin, I wouldn't concern yourselves with it unduly. And I'll figure out what we can do about Lloyd."

With this final parting shot at his superiors, Merthophan took one last stab at dissuading them from caring.

But his words fell on deaf ears. Selen had stood up so fast her chair fell over, moving closer to Choline.

"So if we find the princess, that means we can get Sir Lloyd enlisted?"

"Did you not hear me, Selen Hemein?" Merthophan sighed, rubbing his temples.

Then he saw Riho headed toward Choline with a massive grin.

"Colonel Choline! Tell me more! Just how far does this reward stretch?"

"Riho Flavin...you, too?"

"The Lloyd thing, this bonus, other potentially lucrative side benefits: You expect me to ignore that?"

If Lloyd owed her one, Riho's plans would be that much easier. This was a big wave she had to try and ride.

"Just...don't do anything crazy. Like I said, I don't want to have to clean up after your shit. I'll figure out a way to get Lloyd enlisted that's not dependent on anything as uncertain as locating the princess."

"Ohhhh, the bliss of doing something for Sir Lloyd! And when he comes to thank me, the two of us will...ahhhhhh!"

"Please!" Merthophan wailed.

But Choline just grinned, nodding. "That's the spirit! You find the princess, you'll be sitting pretty, and we'll get someone who can use the meteor rune. Honestly, if we'd known it would take this much time, we should have started with runes to make the flowers bloom or rain fall...I definitely wanna try those out."

All three of them spun around at this last sentence, their voices in sync like a professional chorus.

""""Rain?!""""

"Yep! We found the right rune...come to think of it, why are there ancient runes on this answer sheet again? *Hngg...*"

While she frowned at it, the other three exchanged glances.

"Colonel Merthophan...if this is true, does Sir Lloyd pass?"

"It'll be hard to push it through on the grounds that these *might* be ancient runes...but if it is true, we definitely can't afford to let him slip through our fingers..."

Riho lowered her head, grinning. "He's not just a hidden treasure— he's a bona fide out-of-place artifact. A shaman who can make it rain on demand would be a huge hit, and we'd rake it in..."

Behind his stony face, Merthophan made up his mind.

"Lloyd Belladonna…with him in our army, our military strength is that much more secure…we must have him…"

As for Selen…

"Oh, Sir Lloyd! You wanted to marry me so bad that you even used runes to help you enlist!"

Best to just leave her to it.

Shortly before this all went down, Lloyd had discovered that his number wasn't on the list of admitted candidates and wandered away from the celebrating crowd, head bowed.

"I saw it coming…but it still hurts…"

He'd thought he'd convinced himself he stood no chance, yet part of him had still been hoping against hope.

And now that those hopes had been dashed, he was left staring at the ground, a feeble smile quivering on his lips. He wandered aimlessly through the Central District, not quite up to returning to Marie's house just yet.

This place was filled with military facilities, dorms for soldiers, and shops and bars catering to them. In the center, protected by these facilities, were the homes of the royal family and those connected to them—as imposingly ornate as the military buildings were functional. A striking contrast indeed.

Swept along by military personnel, army school students, merchants, and tourists, he meandered the streets, Lloyd washed up at…

"The military school campus."

The campus was filled with officer cadets. Like any ordinary college, the grounds were open to the public, with benches placed here and there and lots of greenery to admire.

But this was a tough place for Lloyd to be right now. If he'd passed, he might already be here, chatting with new friends…and that thought alone made him sink into a deeper depression.

"I'd better go home. Staying here isn't good for me…"

He turned on his heel…and spied a flyer written in extremely manly handwriting pinned to a bulletin board.

"…Now hiring? …Cooks?"

That handwriting was rough-hewn—manly in a way that might just be *bad*. Lloyd took a step closer, looking it over. It was a job posting for the student cafeteria.

Lloyd thought it through for a minute, then made up his mind and started to walk with purpose. He passed through the flow of the crowd, head high, looking ahead once again.

"—Sorry, everyone back home. I'm gonna be selfish for a little while longer."

His legs carried him to a building that screamed *cafeteria*. Not a restaurant or even a dining hall—definitely way less classy. Like, if it weren't on a campus, the exterior would make you wonder if they even bothered providing chairs. Exactly the sort of place that handwriting had brought to mind.

"Are they closed today?"

The place was certainly quiet. Since they announced the test results today, it would make sense for the cafeteria to be closed. But even if they were open, he wouldn't be surprised to find it like this; nothing about the place suggested business had ever boomed.

Lloyd tried the door, and it swung open. Guess it wasn't locked, then. He stepped inside, hoping someone was there.

"Hello?"

He was welcomed by a floor covered in grease. The interior didn't betray one's expectations, perfectly complementing the gruff exterior of the building. He peered over the counter, but there was no one there. Lloyd was about to give up and go home for the day…

"Who are you?" a voice snarled right behind him, and a fist came flying in his direction.

"Uh, sorry! I didn't mean to…"

As rattled as he was, Lloyd easily dodged the punch—moving so fast that he left an afterimage behind. He didn't appear to be aware that this was anything special, but the man who'd taken a swing at him flashed him a look of surprise.

"What the—?!"

The man froze, fist extended. A burly, square-jawed man. Definitely looked like someone who'd survived more than a few dangerous situations.

His name was Chrome Molybdenum. Former personal guard to the princess.

But Lloyd had no way of knowing that. He just thought the man was unusually well built for a cook.

Chrome Molybdenum. Once the leader of the royal guard, he'd lived for his work.

But for a variety of reasons, he now found himself running a cafeteria. Quite a fall, but this didn't mean he was any less loyal.

He'd come back from an errand to find a strange boy looking around his shop.

And even though he'd been the one to write the job posting, Chrome sensed a power so strong, it never occurred to him that this boy might be a potential candidate—this was why he'd attacked at once.

This boy was a clear threat, so Chrome hadn't hesitated to take a swing...and the boy had dodged it. A bead of sweat ran down the chef's brow.

He resumed a fighting stance, every muscle on his massive frame bulging.

But his body refused to move. Fists raised, he looked Lloyd over, alarm bells blaring through his head.

Who is this kid? ...How can he be so strong that I'd take a swing without even thinking? And strong enough to make me freeze up?

The fact that this stranger had dodged that first swing was proof that Chrome was no match for him. He'd been through enough dangerous situations to know that. Sweat pouring down his face, Chrome's mind spun frantically.

What does he want? Does he know I'm a former royal guard? Does he think he can pry secrets out of me?

Lloyd was just smiling at him. A harmless-looking smile. A natural, honest smile that just scared him even more.

He had to feel this out. With that in mind, Chrome forced himself to speak.

"What brings you here...sir...?"

Lloyd took a breath, trying to speak in slow, even terms. He'd messed up the interview earlier and wanted to answer with as much confidence as he could this time. Sadly, this just helped reinforce Chrome's ideas about him...

"Oh, I found a flyer saying you were hiring."

Chrome snorted. An obvious lie.

He was momentarily surprised, but he's already recovered...he's a pro. To know what he's after...I need to get him to talk.

Keeping his fists raised, Chrome started inching closer, doing his best to match the boy's confidence.

"You don't say? Well, well, this is a cafeteria. What do you bring to the table?"

Lloyd thought about it, then smiled. "I'm great at cooking and cleaning."

"You cook (fools) and clean up (the mess), huh?"

"Not to toot my own horn, but where I'm from, they say I'm the best at it."

"The best (in the crime syndicate), huh?"

This was a breeding ground for misunderstandings.

He's not gonna spill it easily, Chrome decided and lowered his center of gravity, preparing for a hard fight. He had his back to the door—an advantage in this terrain. No matter what, he couldn't let this dangerous assassin leave here alive. He might not be a guard anymore, but his duty was clear.

"Then let's see what you can do," he sneered, keeping the pressure on. He'd inched into range by now.

"Er, well, if that's all it takes, I certainly don't mind!"

Lloyd began rolling up his sleeves, clearly ready to throw down.

"Then...give me your best shot!" Chrome shouted.

"Will risotto work?"

"Uh...sure..."

Even as Chrome's challenge had echoed through the cafeteria, Lloyd had turned and walked into the kitchen, where he started cooking. The way he politely asked "Can I use this?" each time he reached for a new ingredient slowly forced Chrome to lower his fists. Eventually, he took a seat at the counter.

Why is he cooking normally? What's going on?

Chrome's fists might've been lowered, but his guard wasn't. But Lloyd was busy making small talk.

"You see, I actually failed the test to enter the military school..."

"Oh?"

Bullshit, Chrome thought. No way anyone this good could possibly fail.

"And well, everyone in the village saw me off, so I'd feel bad going back home with my tail between my legs...so I thought I'd do what I can to stick around, you know, maybe try the test again next year."

The risotto was starting to smell good, and the sounds of it cooking were making Chrome's stomach growl. Lloyd's smile looked very pleasant.

Chrome listened in silence, frowning.

"I dunno. Maybe the idea that living in the big city will make me better somehow is a super-hick thing to think."

A new thought flicked across the mind behind Chrome's frown.

Huh? Is he just...a normal country kid?

He dismissed the idea at once.

Never! No way! That's what he wants me to think! Look at how he moved! He's no civilian! Keep your guard up!

His fist clenched again.

"Oh," Lloyd said. "I'll need to clean this fish...can I borrow this knife?"

Ngh! So that's your angle? I get it now! Make me let my guard down with this small talk, pretend to clean a fish, and then attack with a knife! A crafty scheme indeed, Chrome thought.

"Um, can I?"

"…Sure," he said, nodding quietly. He would never let the boy know he was on to his scheme.

Just you try. The instant you attack, I'll unleash a counter!

"…Hmm, I thought so. Oh, and would you look at that! The fish in the city don't have horns or fangs! Told you so, Grandpa."

That was a really weird thing to say, but don't let it rattle you, Chrome! Watch his every move!

Chrome steeled himself for battle on his stool.

And shortly after, the meal was ready.

"All done! Risotto."

"Uh, right."

"…………"

"…………"

"…Um, are you gonna try it?"

"………What?"

The beautifully garnished risotto and the tantalizing scent of tomato were really starting to confuse Chrome.

What does this mean? …He's finished the meal!

Chrome looked like the rug had been pulled out from under him, and Lloyd was staring anxiously into his eyes.

"Um…is there something wrong with it? Do you not like tomatoes?"

"No, that's not…oh!"

Chrome suddenly figured it out.

I see! No one lets their guard down more than when they're eating! That's when he's going to strike!

It all fell into place. With that in mind, he took a scoop of risotto and shoved it into his mouth. His eyes locked on Lloyd all the while.

You're on! I'll play your game for now, boy! You'll pay for underestimating the former head of the royal guards!

©Nao Watanuki

*   *   *

And in no time at all, Chrome had finished his meal.

".......""

".......""

".........um."

"...........................huh?"

Lloyd was clearly rattled—presumably because the reaction to the meal had been neither "Good!" nor "Crap!" but "Huh?"

At the same time, Chrome was looking every bit as rattled. He'd eaten the whole thing without event, and the dish had been pretty good. At long last, his mind had begun to entertain another possibility.

.... *Whoa. Is he really just here for a job?*

"Um," Lloyd said anxiously, observing his every expression. "Was it bad?"

"Uh, no, it was pretty good."

This clearly came as a huge relief to the boy. And at last, Chrome finally let his guard down. "So, what's your name?" he asked in a calm voice.

"Oh, sorry! I'm Lloyd Belladonna." The boy bowed politely, which Chrome reciprocated.

"All right. I'm Chrome Molybdenum."

It'd never once occurred to Chrome that the boy might really be here for a job, so he was somewhat at a loss now. Should he really hire someone with this much skill? Even if he didn't have some shadowy syndicate backing him, he was clearly dangerous...and what the hell was Merthophan doing, failing someone like this? What was their test even looking for?

A storm of thoughts swirled through his head, but he eventually settled on, *This boy can't be left out in the field. Best to put him where I can keep an eye on his every move.*

"Lloyd, right? Mm. You're hired."

"Oh! Thank you so much!" Lloyd was clearly genuinely exhilarated.

"But this won't cover room and board. You said you left your hometown, right? You got a place to stay?"

"Yes! Our village chief hooked me up. Er, technically, I'm a freeloader… but I think they'll let me keep on living there, if I can pay for food and the like."

This didn't sound like a lie. Once again, Chrome was forced to take this kid at face value. "Right. And where is that?"

"A small shop in the East Side."

Chrome scratched his chin.

Hmph. If they'd put up with a kid who's this off the charts, they must be even worse…

He never imagined that they were, in fact, the missing princess, the one he was searching for.

Or that Lloyd would lead them to their miraculous reunion.

Meanwhile, back at the Witch of the East Side's place, Alka had spent a good hour threatening to destroy the world, and the princess of the realm, Princess Maria/Marie the Witch, had been desperately trying to stop her.

"Aughhhhhhh! Lloooooooooyd!" Alka wailed.

"Stoppppp, *loli* Grandma! Master dumbass! I mean, you're so adorable today!"

"What the…you can't just add a compliment at the end and hope I forget the insults that proceeded it!"

They'd been going around in circles for nearly an hour. Managing to save the world at last, Marie flopped down on the ground, limbs flung wide, without any trace of regal dignity in sight.

"*Hah…hah…*I just said it was a remote possibility!"

"Oh, my dearest little Lloyd is not that kind of boy! I'm sure that in the end, we'll be united, and he'll return back to my arms, crying, 'Chief! Chief!'"

"You're breaking character… Geez, you dote on him so hard, you can't even let him outta your sight. Why would you ever send him here? Seriously, our army couldn't handle a Kunlun villager."

At this, Alka finally looked serious. "………None of your business, Marie. This is how my heart's desire comes true."

Okay, this is definitely the start of something dumb.

The fake child sitting in front of Marie could wipe out dozens of countries on the slightest of whims. Earthquakes, blizzards, forest fires? Nothing compared to Alka, the walking disaster. She'd yanked around Marie's chain enough times for her to know.

"You can level a mountain for waking up on the wrong side of the bed. What more could you possibly want? If you've got time to dawdle, why not just save the country? Seriously. I kinda mean it."

Marie just tossed this around absently, but Alka smirked and then showed the gravitas befitting a master for the first time.

"Marie…I reckon I've told you this a million times. Me and the villagers in Kunlun only get involved with matters beyond human comprehension—ya know, demon lords or epic disasters. We have no intention of involving ourselves in trifling matters. Human vanity and ensuing wars ain't got nothin' on us."

Says the same person who was ready to destroy the world over an unrequited love.

"Yeah, yeah, I've heard it before. Making these mistakes and regretting the consequences is the only way we can grow, right? And you don't care if that process destroys us. Which is exactly why I worked so hard to learn the *disenchant* rune from you," Marie recalled, staring down at the countless scars on her hands.

"And? Are ya getting anywhere, Princess Maria?"

"Honestly, not really. I believe the king…my father…is being manipulated. And I have information that someone is operating behind the scenes, trying to push public opinion to support the war."

"So the powers behind the scenes are moving."

"Yeah…and with the foundation-day festival coming…many diplomats and heads of state will be visiting, and they'll likely seize that opportunity to make a grand declaration of war. That much I've got, but…"

Alka nodded, deep in thought. "You're no closer to figuring out who's behind this."

"Right. I could force my way into the palace and free my father, but unless I catch the culprit, the same thing is bound to happen again."

Marie kept her face solemn, trying not to let her anxiety and irritation show as she clenched her fists tight.

"And whoever you're against is acting with caution… Ain't there someone in the palace you can trust?"

"My personal guard, Chrome Molybdenum, maybe. But with anyone else, I have no idea who might be connected to who, and I really can't risk identifying myself. And from what I've heard, Chrome is no longer a royal guard."

"I'm hearing you're at a disadvantage with no time to spare, but ya need to do something soon. I reckon that's a lot of responsibility for a fifteen-year-old girl."

Alka acted like it had nothing to do with her, but Marie could sense genuine concern lurking behind her words. That made her even more serious.

"Yeah…I've been afraid to go near the Central District because I might get caught, but I think I'm going to have to go there tomorrow. I can't keep worrying about the consequences." Marie was staring at her hands, her voice grim.

Alka spoke as if trying to convince herself: "Ya know, if there was a demon lord behind this, or a natural disaster, I reckon I'd be happy to help. But as long as it's an internal power struggle…just be careful inside enemy territory, ya hear?"

"I appreciate the warning."

"And let me also say that if you get Lloyd mixed up in this, I'm dragging him back home."

To hide how much this hurt, Marie let her head hang all the way down.

"…I appreciate the warning."

"And I'll have to turn you into a frog for three days. Don't worry, I'll write your suicide note, and I'll make sure to misspell or leave out lots of words to make your suicidal desperation all the more palpable."

"All right, you're leaving *warning* territory and just making threats now! You can't write someone's suicide note for them! That's forgery, you know!"

As Marie shrieked, the door slowly opened to reveal Lloyd, looking guilty, like a kid who'd picked up a stray animal on his way home.

"Oh, welcome back, Lloyd."

"There you aaaaare! Lloooooooyd! It's your beloved chief, Alkaaaaa!" Alka seemed oblivious to Lloyd's mood, as she threw herself at him, wholeheartedly expressing her carnal instincts.

"Hi, wait...why are you here, Chief?"

"Well," *rub, rub*, "you see," *rub, rub*, "I hear my precious Lloyd's results were posted," *pat, pat*, "so I came a-flyin'!" *Gnaw, gnaw.*

"And by fly, she means teleport... Oh, come on! If he's so precious, stop biting him!"

In truth, Alka had been showing up to inquire about him constantly, interrogating Marie without even the excuse of admissions decisions—and devouring Marie's foodstores like a mouse that'd taken up residence in her pantry.

And the teeth marks she left on Lloyd were like rodents gnawing on support pillars.

Lloyd stared at the floor—his expression didn't quite read as embarrassed. "Uh...sorry," he admitted. "I didn't pass."

There was a long silence, and then Alka calmly began writing some runes.

"Cool, then I reckon I'll just destroy this country."

"Please don't! There are children watching!"

"...Oh, good point, good point. I'm kidding, totally kidding, like twenty percent kidding."

"What's the other eighty percent?!"

"Pure spite."

Marie looked as though she could develop an ulcer at any moment from the stress, and Lloyd rubbed her back to cheer her up.

"So, uh...there's something else."

Alka saw how he was fidgeting. "............A woman?" She held up the runes, looking grim.

Clutching her stomach, Marie desperately grabbed Alka's arm.

"Please! Seriously, please! I'll make any silly face you want! I'll grovel before you! For god's sake, don't use that!"

These were the words of the princess of the realm. Lloyd waited for things to calm down before continuing.

"So, uh...I know this is selfish of me, but...I'd like to try the test again next year."

Alka responded with all the dignity of a village chief. "Ah, ya will, of course. I knew that all along, Lloyd."

"You're such a liar!"

Alka ignored this, and Marie glowered at her.

"And I know this is a big favor...but I was hoping I could keep staying here, Marie. I want to get to know the city better, and...I just can't face everyone back home. Oh, but I can pay my share! I got a job!"

"........*You aren't coming home?!*"

"Don't look so horrified, Master. You knew this all along, remember?"

Marie took advantage of Alka's devastation to get a few digs in.

Lloyd turned toward her, bowing his head. "Is that too much to ask, Marie?"

"Uh, no, I'm fine with it. Just..." Marie's face turned slightly red—she was obviously pleased to have him here. But then, rubbing her forehead, she shot a sideways glance at Alka.

But this loli's *gonna jump to conclusions and fight him every step of the way...*

This was Alka they were talking about. She may well decide she'd rather end his life than see him love another woman. Marie readied herself to grovel or make silly faces to soothe Alka's temper tantrums, but the chief was taking it in stride.

"All right...I'll allow it."

Lloyd immediately brightened up.

Marie looked much less sure. "...We might get hit by a meteor tomorrow," she muttered.

"Hmm? Are ya asking me to send one in your direction? Maybe take your whole country down?"

"Please don't!"

Marie was already on her knees, but Alka pulled her to her feet and dragged her to the corner, whispering, "Here's the plan: Solve your case, get back on the throne, and use your power to get Lloyd enlisted, pronto."

"If it were that easy, I'd have done it by now! And why do you want Lloyd to be a soldier so damn bad anyway?"

"All I wanna hear from you is a 'Yes, ma'am.' Do you want me to hit you with that curse for minor misfortunes again? Or should I just skip right to the frog thing? It's been a while."

"Yes! Yes, ma'am!" Marie wailed. "Please don't do the frog thing."

Alka gave her a diabolical grin. "Okay. Then I'll let you off with the minor curse."

"*Loli* Grandma! You didn't say it was a choice!" Marie sounded like a soccer player protesting an unjust foul.

Alka ignored her. "I reckon it's time I got back to work...who knows what those villagers are up to. Anyway, you don't wanna get cursed, solve your problems faster. And, Lloyd! I'll come again!"

And with that, she walked right into the closet. Marie stared after the little devil, sighing.

Meanwhile, Lloyd was just happy he'd been granted permission. He was already in the kitchen, humming like a newlywed. Marie stared at him, rubbing her belly, trying to think.

"...First, I need some medicine for this upset stomach. I'll think later." Preservation of her gastric mucosa was vital. She pulled a wax paper–wrapped bundle from her medicine cabinet and opened it, grumbling, "Geez...next time she tries anything, I'm gonna take the crystal she uses to teleport and bury it at the bottom of a well."

She tossed the medicine in her mouth, and it instantly went down the wrong pipe.

"*Koff! Koff!*"

As she desperately tried to clear it, she stubbed her toe on her desk and fell over. Hearing the crash, Lloyd spun around.

"Marie? Are you...?"

He found her robe flipped up, showing everything underneath—quite the scandalous sight. It was flipped all the way to her neck, so even her enormous chest was exposed like a girl waiting for the doctor to examine her.

"Black... No, I didn't see anything!" Lloyd dashed out of the room like a startled hare, definitely having seen what he shouldn't have.

"............"

Having descended rapidly from princess to witch to...whatever this undignified spectacle was, Marie calmly removed the crystal from her closet and dropped it into her well—totally oblivious to the fact that she'd later come to regret this impulsive action.

A few days later, officer cadets were lined up in a classroom for their entrance ceremony. Sunlight streamed through the window, catching specks of dust in its rays.

If this were a normal entrance ceremony, you'd see a lot of fresh-faced cadets eagerly listening to the words of the speaker, but...Colonel Merthophan had gathered personnel far from innocent. "The incoming class is gonna break my bones. This is gonna be a rough year" was the unanimous opinion of the teaching staff. And on top of that...

"In other words! To serve the troops of the realm! You must strengthen your hearts! And bodies! And hearts!"

Merthophan was delivering this speech with great gusto, making the teachers all the more fearful of the present situation. Of course, the staff was well aware that it was their duty to train the cadets into the best officers, but it worried them to see Merthophan in the wrong frame of mind, especially because he was normally prone to discussing matters in a flat and officious tone. At the moment, he was getting a wee bit carried away—so filled with passion, he didn't even realize that he'd said *hearts* twice.

The biggest inconvenience in this crowd of troublemakers was the infamous one-armed mercenary, Riho, looking incredibly bored in her provided dark green uniform as she listened to the speech.

Merthophan's passionate speech concluded around noon, and with that, the ceremony was over. He stepped off the podium, and Riho darted off after him, catching up to Merthophan as he strode through the schoolyard, surrounded by chattering students. His bolt-upright posture and grim demeanor seemed totally out of place.

"Yo, Boss!" Riho called out like they were old friends. "How's it going?"

"Stop talking to me so casually...," he scolded without bothering to change his expression. "And I'm not your boss. I'm a colonel."

"Yeah, yeah. Geez, guess you've never had a sense of humor."

"What do you want?"

"Well, figured I'd ask if you'd made any progress with the whole Lloyd thing."

"No further developments, unfortunately... We don't even know where he is. He may well have gone back to his village."

There was a hint of regret under his official tone.

He really let a big fish go.

Both of them had sensed something inexplicable from Lloyd. Riho knew all too well how Merthophan felt—although her concern was more about the major blow to her potential income.

"Why involve yourself in his business?" Merthophan asked. "Speaking of, you and Selen both came with me last time... Are you up to something?"

Riho gave him a wink, closing one of her beady eyes and sticking out her tongue. "Tee-hee!"

"So you are."

"Nope, not at all. I just thought, you know, for the sake of the realm, we really should have him enlisted here, yessir."

Of course, Riho's mind was full of ways she could use him for her own financial gain. Helping to get him enlisted would be just another favor for her to cash in on and ride his coattails into the horizon.

"But if we don't know where he is, there's nothing we can do. I've requested they look into it, but..."

"Well, about that. The Belt Princess, um, Selen, was it? Seemed like she had a connection to him, so she might know where he is."

Selen had talked about him like they were bound by fate. If they were as close as she proclaimed, she must know something about his whereabouts.

"Oh? Then we'll know when we ask her." He looked relieved. "Where is she?"

"She booked it outta the building the second the opening ceremony ended. Must be going to see Lloyd or something. See? I don't think we need to worry about finding him."

"Hmm, then the only remaining problem is how we get him enlisted."

"Well, that clearly calls for an abuse of your power, Colonel!"

"…If I set that precedent, the fools above me will exploit the hell out of it to foist their families on me… Are you trying to fill the army with inept soldiers?"

"Yeesh, that sounds like a pain. Maybe not that, then," she recanted under his sharp glare.

"After lunch, I'm going to see what I can do… You coming, Riho Flavin?"

"Oh? Is that an invitation?"

"Yes. I'm going to meet up with a man. It won't hurt you to know the fella," Merthophan added.

That sounded significant. She cocked her neck to the side, uncertain of what he could be up to. Merthophan tromped forward as he answered her unspoken question.

"He's a former royal guard. Now he runs a cafeteria for the cadets: The kind of place where the portions are huge, the price is right, and the flavor is questionable at best."

"He had one job! He's failing at the single most important part."

"See, he insists if it tastes too good, it'll ruin them for field rations. And the shop itself is always a bit dirty—you know, greasy floors and the like. Most students seek out the fancier dining hall instead."

"Um, sounds like he should be focusing less on business practices and more on preventing the whole place from shutting down. I mean, as soon as the health inspector arrives…"

"...According to him, a real soldier will eat no matter how dirty their location."

Riho was starting to lag behind. *This was a mistake*, she thought. But the cafeteria was already in sight.

"That's odd. There's usually less people here."

Despite the colonel's official review, business seemed to be booming. When they stepped inside, they found a place that might be a little old, but was spick-and-span—the sort of place that had the potential to generate long lines.

"Not as dirty as you described... You sure this isn't the dining hall?"

"...No...did he revamp the place? With what money?"

Two seats at the counter had opened just as they stepped in, so they sat down together. In front of them, a grim-looking man—apparently the owner—was busily cleaning fish. Chrome glanced up, recognized them, and grunted, "Merthophan...what do you want?"

"What do you think? You're still running a cafeteria, aren't you, Chrome?" he curtly replied with a question, but they were clearly old friends. Merthophan ordered the usual.

"...And you?"

"Uh...the risotto."

"Comin' right up," he announced and lumbered into the kitchen.

The second Chrome was out of sight, Riho leaned in, whispering in Merthophan's ear. "Colonel, that guy's seriously skilled. He ain't just a former royal guard, is he?"

"...Well. He was the head guard: He personally guarded the princess."

"The head of the royal guards... What's someone like that doin' in a cafeteria?"

"One thing led to another... But I'll get him to teach for us one of these days. All he has to do is say yes... Either way, he's worth knowing."

She wanted to pry further about this "one thing" that led him to this job, but Chrome came back with a pile of risotto, a pasta dish slathered in meat sauce, and two salads with a heap of croutons.

"Oh, that looks good," Riho commented.

"Hmm… You been training, Chrome?"

"Shut up and eat."

He put the food down and turned his attention toward the sink, busying himself with washing dishes impassively. Riho took a bite of her risotto and went bug-eyed the moment she tasted it.

She glared at Merthophan. "Were you lying to me?"

"No." He was stone-facedly slurping pasta. "That *is* good," he muttered, licking his lips.

"The food here's real good."

"Mm."

"And they're using quality rice! These tomatoes aren't cheap, either."

"Mm." Merthophan frowned, wiping his mouth, and looked at Chrome. "Chrome, what's going on? The food is *good*!"

"Who complains about good food?" Chrome snarled, still wrestling with the dishes. The shop was never this crowded, and he was struggling to keep up with the volume.

Merthophan was unconvinced, speaking gruffly. "You never gave a damn about seasoning or the quality of your ingredients! You're making me look like a liar here!" He took a gulp of his tea. "Hey!" he roared. "What's going on?! Even the tea is good!"

It was completely illogical for a man to get angry about an enjoyable meal. Chrome stopped washing dishes and turned to glare at him.

"So what if it is? Good food, good tea! What else do you want from a cafeteria?"

"And look at the floor! Where's the grease?! It's practically spotless!"

"You're gonna complain about clean floors now? Don't tell me you actually liked that slimy mess!"

"Oh geez. It's over when even the owner admits it's greasy…," Riho muttered, sipping her tea.

Chrome scowled at her but calmed down a little. "…I hired a new guy," he admitted.

"You're telling me someone agreed to help at a filthy shop run by an unpleasant boss? Is he a monk seeking enlightenment?!"

"Merthophan...I really don't know what you saw in this place..."

The assertion that working here must be a form of spiritual training left Chrome rubbing his temples. But the commotion must have attracted the attention of his new hire, because he poked his head out of the kitchen.

"Boss? What's up?"

And the moment they saw the new hire—Lloyd—both Merthophan and Riho did a spit take with their highly regarded cups of tea.

Lloyd started to glance their way, but someone at another table called out, ready to order.

"Coming!"

He bowed his head at Riho and Merthophan without really looking at them and scampered off to take the order. Once he recovered somewhat, Merthophan started grilling Chrome, leaning so far on the counter that if Choline had been there, she'd have warned him about breaking character. Imagine an excited child trying to clamber up onto a table. Yep. That's it.

"What's going on, Chrome?! Why is he working here?!"

"What?! You know who he is, Merthophan?"

"Not at all!"

"Hey!"

What's with this conversation? Riho wiped her mouth with a paper napkin, shaking her head at the two older men.

"Chrome, don't tell me your senses have dulled so much you can't tell who you're dealing with."

"You idiot! I may have been out of the field for a while, but there's no way I'd miss his inexplicable force—first time I've ever sat there fearing for my life while someone cooked me a goddamn meal!"

Then it was Chrome's turn to lean in, bombarding Merthophan with questions of his own.

"Could it be that your senses have dulled, Merthophan? How could a beast like that fail your test?"

"...That's a sore spot of mine." Merthophan took his turn rubbing his temples.

©Nao Watanuki

"Anyway, he can cook, he can clean, why wouldn't I hire him? …And you can't let someone like that slip through your fingers. I thought he was an enemy agent at first."

"…Even if he isn't, best not to let the wrong people get their hands on him. Good call, Chrome." Merthophan gave Riho a sideways glance.

She whistled, feigning innocence, as she looked quickly away from him.

"Haven't seen anything suspicious from him. He says he needs the job to earn his keep until the test next year… Didn't seem like he was lying."

As Chrome spoke, Lloyd called out from the back. "Hey, Boss! Where do we toss the trash?"

"There's a dumpster out back!"

"Right!" Lloyd replied and stepped outside.

"He's a hard worker, nice enough, good with customers…and like just now, perceptive."

Merthophan bowed his head. "Do you mind looking after him awhile longer? I'm gonna see what strings I can pull to make him a cadet."

"Even Mr. Rules-and-Regulations over here will make exceptions for someone like him, huh… Got it. I'll keep him here as if my life depends on it."

"……I'll owe you one."

Riho watched them with a frown. …*I'm sorry. This* is *a cafeteria, right?*

This foreboding conversation certainly didn't sound like it was taking place in one.

Just then, sounds of a commotion rang outside.

"What is that? Some sort of fight?" Riho perked up her ears. From the chatter of passersby, she caught the words *fight*, *powder keg*, and *Belt Princess*.

…Belt Princess? What is she *up to?*

After she exchanged a quick word with the foreboding duo, they all went to check out the source of the commotion.

*   *   *

"—What do you mean by that?" called out a voice.

Riho started to book it toward the scene, where Selen and Allan were arguing with each other.

"—I dunno what you're thinking, Princess. But if you drag the name of the local lords through the dirt again, it's a problem for me."

The main path in the academy was crowded with cadets, soldiers, tourists, and deliverymen. And in the dead center of it all, a crowd was starting to form around the two cadets.

"...What do you want? I'm busy." Selen shot Allan a look of contempt through her fluttering blond hair.

He kept talking, undeterred. "What do you think? I hear you're looking for someone all over town and making trouble everywhere you go!"

"They were the ones who picked a fight with me," the blond girl stated. "They said they'd seen Lloyd, and when I followed them, it turned out they had vulgar intentions, so I inflicted some pain on them." There wasn't a flicker of doubt in her eyes.

"Why you... You aren't stopping at damaging the rep of the lords, huh? Are ya gonna ruin the rep of all the cadets while you're at it, too?"

"I hardly did anything that would damage anyone's 'rep.' It wasn't a big deal. I just tore some chest hair off that man."

"Holy! That's a big deal! It'll sting when he takes a bath!"

"—Fine, next time someone tries something, I'll go for their arm hair instead."

"What have you got against body hair?! Plus, it's hard to even sleep at night once you notice stubble all over your skin!"

The argument seemed to be veering off track, but Selen locked eyes with Allan, glaring at him and not backing down, as the heat increased in their discourse on body hair.

"Either way, anyone gets in the way of Sir Lloyd and me, I will show them no mercy."

Allan grinned as if he'd been waiting to hear those words. "You said it. If this mess goes on any longer, it'll affect my chances at gettin' a promotion... I'm gonna have to show *you* no mercy, Belt Princess."

"My name's Selen... And it sounds like you want to find out what you look like bald."

"That's not body hair! That's a vital part of me!"

They were hitting a strange tenor somewhere between goofy and menacing, but the moment both drew their weapons, the needle shot straight to maximum tension.

"Don't worry...I won't swing all the way through," Allan consoled, stroking the edge of his battle-ax: a two-headed, elaborately decorated weapon. If he did swing all the way, the results would be fatal.

".........Suit yourself." Selen held her rapier aloft, looking completely unconcerned. Following the custom, she was ready to tap her weapon against his.

But Allan did no such thing. With a speed belying his size, he closed the distance between them.

Caught off guard by his speed, Selen reacted too late.

"You lack experience, Princess!"

"Hngg!"

But just as the ax was almost upon her...

There was a snap, and the cursed belt around Selen's waist stopped Allan mid-swing.

"Huh?"

It batted the blade, moving as if it were alive—but a moment later, it coiled back around her waist. The movement of the crimson belt was so uncanny that a hush fell over the crowd.

"Wait, wait, what's with that belt?! It moved!"

"Yes. It's—you know! It's a boon that Sir Lloyd granted me!"

"Huh? That doesn't even make sense!"

"I'm trying to say it's that thing that happens all the time! It's an age-old tale: A gift from a loved one that the main character keeps in their pocket saves them when an arrow hits them in the exact same spot—!"

"Oh wow, how nostalgi— I mean, hey! It's not in your pocket! And it definitely moved! ...Is that a belt or a snake?!"

"I'm trying to say my life belongs to Lloyd! This belt is the red string of destiny!" She rubbed her cheek against it, and the crowd shuddered at this sight. Selen really knew how to work a crowd.

"*Tch,* whatever." Allan raised his ax again, lowering his stance with murder in his eyes. "I'll just have to cut through you and your creepy belt…no more holding back."

A chilling statement for sure. The witnesses gulped, certain they were about to see blood—until one boy tromped by, clutching a pile of garbage, seemingly oblivious to the tense scene.

"Oh, sorry, I thought I heard my name," Lloyd explained, his tone utterly relaxed. He was carrying a LOT of garbage.

"What? We didn't call a sanitation worker," Allan spat.

Lloyd lowered the trash to the ground, looking from one to the other. "Uh, no, I'm not…I'm Lloyd Belladonna…"

"Sir Lloyd!"

There was a gust of wind as Selen dived at him. Lloyd appeared to be every bit as lost as Allan. Every jaw in the crowd dropped, too.

"Oh, Sir Lloyd! You saw I was in danger and came to save me, right? The two of us are destined—"

For all this time, Selen had been searching high and low for him, and from her perspective, it seemed her fated lover had jumped in to save her just as a dangerous man was trying to attack her. Her feelings—er, delusions—were practically leaking out of her brain for all to see. Left to her own devices, she was likely to rattle on about their future together till death did they part.

Once he'd dutifully listened to her delusions, Lloyd obeyed her rambling wishes, asking Allan, "Uh, you were putting her in danger? Should I fight you in her place…?"

"Uh, no…um…"

Lloyd's chilled-out tone and Selen's excessively cheerful PDA seemed to rob Allan of his anger.

"So you're the Lloyd that Selen was looking for? You work at the cafeteria, right?"

Well, if she's found him, maybe she'll stop making trouble… Allan stashed his weapon.

©Nao Watanuki

"Um…"

"Oh, don't worry, kid. I may be a cadet, but I'm still a soldier. We don't go around attacking civilians. And it looks like the matter is settled for now. Hey, Belt Princess! I'll let you off this time, but you cause any more trouble, I won't show any mercy!"

"Oh, Sir Lloyd, Sir Lloyd, Sir Lloyd!"

"She's not listening…"

A moment later, Choline came running over, catching wind of the commotion.

"Oy! What's goin' on?! Allan, Selen, they said you were fixin' to throw down! …What the heck is *that*?!" She pointed at Selen, who was busy rubbing her cheek all over Lloyd's chest.

Allan snapped to attention and explained the situation.

"—and that's the long and short of it. The problem's solved for now."

"Riiiight…well, at least it didn't turn into anything major. Huh. *Lloyd?* I feel like I've heard that name before…where was it…?"

While Choline was searching her memories, Merthophan & Co. finally arrived to the scene. The crowd parted before him.

"What's all the fuss?" His dispassionate gravitas was enough to silence the crowd of onlookers, who were mostly students.

Choline was the first to answer. "Oh! Merthophan! And Riho and… Chrome?!"

She was clearly surprised by this last one.

"What's going on, Choline?"

"Uh, long story short, Allan and Selen were fighting, but this Lloyd kid stopped them."

""Lloyd?!""

In response to this chorus, Selen finally pulled her face out of his chest and launched into a passionate explanation. "Exactly! To protect me! To stand in my stead! To fight this brute of a man!"

"…Says the woman running around town ripping people's chest hair out," Allan grumbled. But nobody was listening to him.

"What are you thinking?" Riho asked.

Merthophan grunted. "Riho Flavin...you must know. With everything you've experienced on the battlefield...you must be able to estimate his strength."

Riho shot him a look, clearly stating she had no idea why he was bringing this up now.

"If Lloyd were to fight...," Merthophan continued, "he'd have a chance to prove his power... Wouldn't you want to see that?"

Realization dawned on her. At a glance, Lloyd looked like he couldn't even hurt a fly—she'd doubted her own instincts when she'd met him for the first time.

"Yeah, I could stand to see him in action..."

Riho was mostly in it for the money, but sheer curiosity took its place this time.

"If he thoroughly defeats Allan...that might help my grounds to get him enlisted," Merthophan muttered. He took a few steps over to Allan. "Is that true? Are you really willing to fight this Lloyd kid?"

Allan snapped his heels together, saluting. He shook his head. "No, sir. We've settled the problem in question...and I consider myself a soldier, sir. I wouldn't dream of laying a finger on an innocent civilian."

"Take a hint."

"Huh?"

While Allan was playing the part of a model soldier, Merthophan gave him a serious look...no, more like a pointed glare. Allan had no idea what he'd done to incur the colonel's wrath, so he just stood there, mouth agape.

"You're a soldier! And you're telling me you can't even beat up a mere civilian?!" he roared.

The crowd gasped in horror, and Choline quickly jumped in.

"Wait, Merthophan! You always say, 'Soldiers exist to protect civilians, not harm them!' You're acting very strange lately."

"......"

"Why won't you meet my eye?!"

Merthophan looked guilty for a second, then leaned in and whispered, "Choline, this *Lloyd* over here is the ancient-rune kid."

".........." With that, Choline marched right on over to the center of the crowd.

"Fighters, ready?" she yelled.

She'd volunteered to be the referee, quickly setting the scene with spirited vibrato.

Meanwhile, Allan was utterly at a loss. He'd said all the right things, only to be yelled at and thrown into a fight. He was just about ready to burst into tears.

What's going on? Why do the colonels want me to fight?

He searched desperately for any kind of explanation.

And reached his conclusion: *...gh! Oh! Duh! They know I'm from the house of Lidocaine, known for their militaristic feats; they've heard of my victories in tournaments! They want to see what I can do!*

(Doesn't his optimism bring a tear to your eye?)

Allan spun around to face Lloyd and bowed apologetically. "Sorry, kid. Mind going against me?"

"Huh? M-me? But I'm not that strong," Lloyd stammered.

Allan bowed his head even lower. "Please...I've got plans, and I need to prove myself. Could you grant me this chance?"

"U-uh...but...okay, then."

"Oh! Thank you, young sport!"

And thus, a battle began despite no one in the crowd having the slightest clue why. The soldier and the part-timer were being downright deferential, exclaiming "Thank you!" and "Not at all!" They were about to start a match that no one asked for nor really cared about.

Yet, Merthophan was one of the most powerful men in the army, and Choline the resident magic expert, and they were both staring the pair down like they were afraid to blink. All of this was creating a very strange mood at the battle scene.

To have a man as powerful as the colonel demand to see me fight? I can't waste this opportunity! I've got to show him what I can do!

Allan was getting himself fired up, but the two colonels were muttering to themselves.

"…Hurry up." *Mutter.*

"Show me these runes!" *Mumble.*

They were all clearly after very different things. But Allan was oblivious to this, taking a few steps forward and brandishing his ax.

"My name is Allan Toin Lidocaine. Eldest son of the heavily decorated Lidocaine household…"

He started making a speech that no one wanted to hear—though an amusing error for anyone who knew what was going on.

Once his introduction finally came to a close, it was time for a fight. That was when Allan noticed Lloyd was unarmed.

"Um, ready when you are," Lloyd announced.

"Wait a sec. You're unarmed."

"Uh, yes."

"Hmm…well, I can hardly fight an unarmed man. Someone get him a—"

Choline shot him a glare. "Take a hint!"

"Uh…"

Another harsh rejection. This one was equally inexplicable. Allan started to well up with tears.

"…He don't need no weapons when he has runes—," Choline muttered under her breath.

But Allan had no way of knowing what she was after and remained confused, through and through.

Meanwhile, on the outskirts of the spectators, Riho had slipped up beside Merthophan.

"Uh, Merthophan," she whispered.

"What?"

"Allan…might seriously get himself killed here."

"No, I doubt that. He may not look it, but he's won a number of tournaments—he's a skilled fighter. Has a reputation for being able to take a hit, too."

Chrome stepped in. "Not only that, young lady, but Choline is an expert on magic…particularly recovery spells. She can easily heal a few minor injuries."

"You don't say? …I find it hard to believe."

In the center of the crowd, the expert-in-question was screeching, "Fight now or you'll both see blood!"

It reeeeeeeally seemed like she was on the other end of the injury equation.

"…You sure?"

"…Yeah, she's saved both me and Merthophan," Chrome explained, pretending he hadn't heard Choline at all.

"Mm, as long as he doesn't die instantly, it'll be fine," Merthophan insisted. "…Yeah, it really shouldn't be an issue as long as Allan doesn't take a blow direct to the face unguarded."

"Well, let's just hope we don't see his face turn into tomato puree."

Just as everyone watching got on the same page, Allan had a great idea.

"Right! I've gotta give you some sort of advantage!"

"Y-you do?" Lloyd looked confused.

"Yep. Can't have this fight be too one-sided! I'll…let you take the first swing! Go on—hit me in the face as hard as you can! Tough is my middle name!"

"Uh, o-okay…I'll do what I can."

"That's the spirit! Don't hold back! Come on!"

"…Merthophan?"

"…He's a goner."

"Hey!" Chrome roared. "Why are you just standing there! I'll stop them! Or you'll never be able to eat tomatoes again!"

At this, the two officers snapped back to reality, leaping forward to stop the public execution. As they sprinted toward the battle scene, Lloyd's fist was swinging toward the side of Allan's face at full power.

"Here it goes!"

""""Don't go (meet your maker)!!""""

It was the moment before the ripened tomato was about to explode into smithereens…a gust of wind sprang up from Allan's feet.

"Huh?" "Er…what?" "Eek!" "Oy!"

The wind lifted up dust and garbage and skirts—blinding everyone crowding around the scuffle.

At last, the wind died down. Riho and Selen rubbed their eyes and took in the scene in front of them.

"He's gone?"

There was no sign of Lloyd at all. They looked around, dazed and confused.

"Auuuughhh! Who cast that wind spell? You knocked my hook undone!"

Choline had been right in the middle of the gale, and it had unfortunately undone the hook of her pencil skirt, knocking it straight to the ground. The result was undignified. (I shall spare you the details—but I think it's sufficient to say "it" was beige.)

"Choline? What was that? An enemy attack?"

"The spell wasn't that powerful… Just your everyday wind magic. But Merthophan…did ya see?"

"Where Lloyd Belladonna went? No."

Choline had hastily put her skirt back on and seemed all the more irritated by Merthophan's oblivious response.

"Not that! Under my skirt! …If I'd known this would happen, I'd have picked my favorite, not the discount three-pack."

The last line was under her breath, and Merthophan couldn't make out a word.

He tried to move on, using the worst possible phrasing.

"No one cares about that! What matters here—"

There was an audible snap as veins pulsed on Choline's brow, and she snarled, "…Hey. Choose your words wisely, stone-face. I'm advising you to sugarcoat it: Hint that you wanted to see them and dejectedly insist you missed your chance."

"That is a rather tall order, Choline. Where that boy went is of far greater..."

"Nope. This point needs to be driven home! You need to understand how a woman's mind—"

"S-stop! Choline! Assess the situation!"

Across the crowd, Chrome had seen anything but pantics. In the swirling winds, he'd spied not beige but a girl in witchy black clothing with a pointy hat... And her profile looked awfully familiar...

"The princess...? Was that the princess?" He pushed through the crowd, hurrying after the retreating figure.

"Hey, Chrome! Chr...Chrome! Come back! Help! Augh!"

Merthophan's death throes echoed in his ears, but Chrome paid them no heed.

On a roof of a military building far off from the main path, Marie was heaving, Lloyd clasped under one arm.

"*Hah*...that was a close one..."

Marie had sneaked into the Central District, risking exposure, to sniff out some intel and stumbled upon the scene of a public execution. Sweat seeped out of every pore in her body now that she allowed herself to be relieved.

As for Lloyd...

"I see...you stepped in to stop me getting beat to a pulp!"

...he was wrong once again. But he'd spoken so softly, Marie didn't hear him.

She put Lloyd down and assumed her best scolding expression, as though she were her older sister.

"What were you thinking, Lloyd? That could have been fatal!"

For the other guy! But before she could clarify, Lloyd bowed his head low, hastily apologizing.

"I'm really sorry! Thanks so much for saving me! I owe you my life! I'll do anything to make up for it!"

Then he just looked at her, eyes glistening. Lloyd's puppy-dog act and entirely *on-brand* misunderstandings were enough to make Marie abandon the idea of getting angry. She'd raised a finger at him, and unsure what to do with it, she settled for poking his forehead.

"But you're always so uncertain, so I have to admit I was surprised to see you fighting... What happened?"

"Um, just...going with the flow? I didn't know what I could really accomplish there, but...he asked nicely?"

That's the vaguest reason I've ever heard, Marie thought, exasperated. "Okay, then. When you aren't sure what you can do, it's important to take that step forward. Mm."

That sounded conclusive enough. And Lloyd took it as profound.

"Th-that's true...I'll try and keep taking those steps!"

His smile was just too pure, and Marie blushed despite herself.

"You can't just agree to anything willy-nilly, though! Or bad people might pull one over on you... Women like me, for instance."

"Huh? But you're super nice!"

"...........Geez."

He might be the one pulling one over on her. With flushed cheeks in response to his genuine praise, she put her arms around him—perhaps intentionally a little too close—and jumped down off the roof with him.

Her wind spell softened their landing in the alley. She glanced around.

"Good, nobody here."

"Mm? Would it be bad if there was?"

"N-no! Never mind, just forget I said anything."

In a deserted space between buildings, in a dimly lit path—Alka would probably scream, "I reckon this here is the perfect opportunity!"

No, no, that's not me! Just because he said he'd do anything...or was that an invitation? A sign from god? No, calm down! You're a princess! You can't go acting like some silly little girl...!

As Marie tried to shake off her fantasies, a large man appeared behind her, out of breath.

"Um...you there!"

"N-no! I'm not doing anything wrong!" she yelped, obviously suspicious...but then she recognized his face and immediately recovered. "Chrome...?"

That square frame and sharp jaw appeared out of the darkness... wearing an apron that didn't suit him at all—Marie's former royal guard and trusted confidant, Chrome Molybdenum.

When Lloyd took notice of this newcomer, he dashed over to him, bowing his head. "Boss! S-sorry! A lot happened while I was taking out the trash!"

"Uh...boss?" she asked.

Chrome had been gaping at Marie, stunned to find the missing princess at long last. When he heard Lloyd, he did his best to shake off his confusion, clearing his throat as he calmed himself down.

"*Ahem*...that's fine, Lloyd. More importantly...Lady Maria."

Lloyd blinked. "Huh? No, erm, Boss. This is Marie. She's the witch who's been helping me out."

"Mm? Marie? Helping you out?"

This was getting them nowhere. Marie scrunched Lloyd's hair between her fingers. "You can explain that later, Lloyd. Aren't you supposed to be at work?"

"Oh, right. There's no one minding the shop," Chrome tacked on.

"Oh no! I'll head right back!" Lloyd yelped and vanished with the wind.

Chrome and Marie watched him go. Then it was time to take advantage of their chance encounter.

"Nice to see you again, Chrome. It's been...what, five years?"

"That long? I'm relieved to see you safe. I, Chrome Molybdenum, have been worried sick by your absence." He took a knee before her.

"Oh, Chrome! Don't. On your feet. I can't have anyone seeing us...I have to keep my identity on the down low."

"Your identity? But why...? I see, that explains the fake glasses."

"It's a long story... Can we meet again soon? I'll fill you in then."

"Understood. I'll meet you tonight behind the cafeteria." With a bow, he took his leave.

Marie watched him go, drawing in a deep breath to get her head back in the game.

Finding Chrome was a happy accident...all thanks to Lloyd, again. This should be a huge step forward.

She glanced through the gaps in the mildewy buildings, zeroing in on the castle looming over the town. Her eyes narrowed.

The international leadership conference at the foundation-day festival... that's my D-Day. I have to find the culprit and free my father before then...

Facing the castle, she clenched her scarred hands.

...by using this disenchant rune!

The campus of the military academy was dark and quiet after nightfall. A few lights carried by patrolling guards swayed before vanishing into buildings.

But the cafeteria remained open with its windows aglow. The sound of hushed voices came from out back where two shadows were talking quietly.

One silhouette was Chrome, his square frame stuffed awkwardly into an apron—and the other was Marie, the Witch of the East Side/ the alleged missing princess, Maria.

"I see...someone's controlling the king, but he managed to send you away before losing total control of his thoughts... That must have been hard on you."

Marie had finished recounting her story from the time of the incident until the present day (with a TON of griping about Alka in between). Chrome nodded gravely.

"Yes...and until we know the mastermind behind all this, I can't risk taking any direct action. I could burst into the castle and free my father, but the moment we let our guard down, we'll both be under their control again."

Gazing up at the moonlit castle, Chrome explained how he'd been reduced to running a cafeteria. "After you went missing, His Majesty's behavior changed dramatically. He began backing the war hawks, fanning the flames of battle…and showed himself in public less and less."

"That's what everyone in town has been telling me. The rumors stand true."

"I thought something was up. That was why I took personal responsibility for losing track of you, using that as an excuse to retire and lie low while running this cafeteria—searching for the missing princess and the reason behind His Majesty's transformation."

"And because we were both hiding our true identities, neither of us could find the other…"

"Thankfully, Lloyd brought us together."

His name brought them back to the scene of the attempted murder.

"That reminds me! Why didn't you stop Lloyd, Chrome? A second later, and I'd never have been able to eat chilled tomatoes or organ-meat stew ever again!"

To Chrome's ears, this sounded like pub food, but he let that pass without comment, bowing his head apologetically.

"I have no excuse. Part of me wanted to see the true nature of his strength…"

"And seeing that would have resulted in that man's death… Although I suppose I can understand where you're coming from—like a morbid curiosity."

"Who is he anyway? Why is he with you?"

Marie stared into the darkness. "Have you heard the legends of Kunlun?"

"Uh… The old stories? Where the heroes of yore founded a town far from the rest of the world? Where they live in peace?"

These tall tales were about the descendants of legendary heroes, scholars, and generals who saved the world from disasters and would-be demon lords. According to legend, they congregated in a town called Kunlun. But these stories were full of nonsense—mountains flowing with human souls, multigenerational legendary swords and armor that could protect you from any monster attacks, a village surrounded by treants, a river filled with killer piranhas. Chrome had never believed a word of it.

And Marie spoke as if these works of fiction had something to do with her. "I'd rather not speak of it at all...but Kunlun really exists. My master is the chief there."

"You mean that?"

"I wish I didn't... But she can vaporize demon lords with one hand, teleport wherever...I've seen firsthand her absurd amounts of power."

"Whew...," Chrome uncharacteristically responded.

Marie gave him a sideways look before tacking on an even more shocking truth: "Lloyd's from Kunlun. He's related to my master somehow."

"Whew..."

"I spent years learning to master the *disenchant* rune, and he uses it like it's nothing. He thinks monsters are just wild animals... You heard about the locust that appeared in town? He's the one who killed it without anyone noticing. To top it all off, he said, 'There's more bugs in the city than I expected!' He's a good kid, but dear god."

Chrome had run out of ways to react.

"That's about all I can tell you. Just...don't use him for evil."

"I wouldn't dare. He's been a big help with the cooking and cleaning."

"And keep it secret, please. My master always said, 'My people must never be involved in the affairs of man—only with natural disasters or the schemes of demon lords.'"

"I'll bear that in mind."

"Which means we can't get Lloyd mixed up in this mess, or she'll drag him back home. And that would be the end of his dream."

"I'll bear that in mind."

"Break that promise, and you'll get turned into a frog... Have you ever been turned into one? Oh, it's horrible: If you haven't mastered cutaneous respiration, you can barely breathe. Plus, your skin dries out in minutes. After my first time, I make sure to pour some water on all the frogs I pass by...ah-ha-ha," she ended in a hollow laugh.

"I'll bear that in mind even more."

He didn't know what else to say.

"At any rate, I could use your help, Chrome... But Lloyd is gonna start getting worried, so I'd better head back."

At this, Chrome's expression softened, looking like a brother wishing for his little sister's happiness.

Marie picked up on this and hastily added, "N-not like that! Don't get the wrong idea! A-anyway, keep this a secret! That includes your two friends."

"I won't tell them... Even if I did, I dunno if they'd believe me. But I've known them a long time. They can be trusted."

Chrome glanced inside the warmly lit windows of the cafeteria. They could hear raised voices coming from the back; he could vaguely make out his name in the mix.

"All right," Marie said. "Your friends are calling you. I'd better get home."

Chrome watched Marie until she vanished into the darkness and then went back inside, heading for the heart of the commotion... Merthophan was plastered, and when he saw Chrome, he waved a glass.

"Where were you, Chrome?! A soldier must be swift!"

"Yeah! Were you on the can?!" Choline asked.

The cafeteria was already closed for the night. But whenever anything happened, the two of them would come here to drink, making themselves at home.

Merthophan was piss drunk already, leaning against the table with flushed cheeks in a way that he'd never do if he were sober. He'd never embarrass himself in front of anyone but his closest friends, and Chrome had long since grown used to it.

"...Sorry. Here, have some smoked meat."

He grumpily dropped a plate of meat off in front of them, and Merthophan dived into it like an excited child, stuffing his mouth full. If any of his subordinates had seem him like this, they would definitely have cringed.

"Oh! The flavor! It's not too good! Chrome, you made this, right?"

"...Yeah, yeah, point taken."

Chrome brushed him off, but now it was Choline's turn.

"Whew, Chrome, your part-timer's the best! His food could easily be served in a restaurant, and it wouldn't seem out of place!"

"…This is a restaurant, so it's not out of place."

"Oh, right! I keep forgetting, given how deserted this place has always been."

"…Yeah, yeah, point taken."

Chrome knew they'd continue late into the night once they were like this, and he'd let himself have a few drinks with them. But he couldn't really get drunk since he was on the clock. This went on for a good hour before Merthophan finally blurted out the thing he'd been wanting to say all along.

"Anyway, to find Lloyd Belladonna working here…and what was that? There was a sudden gust of wind, and then he was gone in the next moment."

"…I asked him, and he said he got too scared to fight and ran away when it picked up."

This was a lie, of course.

Choline gave him a look of suspicion, and the smell of booze trailed after her words. "He diiid? Or are ya hiding something? He's not, like, the descendant of some legendary hero who suddenly hesitated to show off his real power or whatever, right?"

Awfully close to the mark, there…

Choline's instincts could be uncanny. Chrome rubbed his forehead.

"…The Belt Princess said, 'Sir Lloyd is wonderful and hates unnecessary bloodshed!'" Merthophan added. "Such a shame. The perfect chance to see what he could really do—wasted!"

Chrome jumped on this, hoping Choline would forget her suggestion. "B-but, Merthophan! That Allan boy could have very well died!"

"…Uh…you have a point there…"

"Still, I know you have your reasons for wanting better personnel," Chrome continued.

Choline took this as a loaded statement. She peered into his face, her face red. "What? Something I don't know?"

Merthophan took a quaff of amber-colored liquor, then answered her.

"You see, a long time ago, there was a famine. The Jiou forces wound up stealing all the stockpiles from my hometown. If our army had been just a little larger, we could have increased patrols on the border...I won't let that happen again."

"So that's why you're recruitin' anything with a rep? And why you're so into Lloyd... Oh, and why you're making us research runes, even though only the princess has a hope of using 'em."

"We need every advantage in a war against Jiou. I'll do whatever it takes to win...whatever it takes." He upended his glass, letting the contents pour into his mouth. Then he let out a boozy sigh, and a look of sadness crossed his face.

An alcoholic ennui settled over the table. In an effort to break out of it, Choline changed the subject.

"Right! Speaking of the princess, rumor has it that she's been spotted in the Central District!"

"*Ka-hack!*" coughed Chrome, who'd just been speaking to the person in question. He managed to splutter, "Y-you don't say?"

Ignoring his flustered state, Choline pressed on. "So people are talking about making another hard push to find her."

"Really? Splitting our forces as we're at the peak of preparing for the foundation-day festival?" Merthophan grumbled, trying to prop his chin up on one hand.

"Not like they ain't aware of that. We can't exactly have the Jiou capturing the princess and holding her hostage, can we? People are sayin' these monsters showing up in town are their way of trying to kill her."

"...The anti-war faction is just trying to get the princess on their side to argue against the king... Waste of everyone's time," Merthophan muttered.

Choline sighed. "*Hah*... Also, there's rumors that the princess is the one secretly takin' these monsters down. Well, that much is clearly just a rumor..."

"*Ka-haaaack!*"

Chrome's coughing fit was so loud this time, Merthophan finally had to acknowledge it.

"Are you getting sick on us, here? Getting frail in your dotage?"

"M-maybe…"

Chrome wasn't coughing because of any illness, but because he knew it was Lloyd who'd taken care of the monsters. Without ever realizing he was fighting monsters, to boot—he'd killed them the same way you'd squash bugs that cross your path. Yet, that had led the whole town to buzz about the hero who'd sought no reward.

Meanwhile, Merthophan sullenly refilled his cup, guzzled it down, and continued making his feelings clear.

"Point is, we need to focus on the foundation-day festival and preparing for war with Jiou. The princess's safety is low on the priority list… Unless, of course, Princess Maria is willing to use her knowledge of runes to lead the forces against Jiou."

"…I might have a problem there, Merthophan," Chrome glowered. "You want the princess getting her hands dirty?"

Merthophan raised his voice, sticking to his guns. With the booze lending wind to his sails, all traces of his usual professionalism were gone out the window.

"Only reason the Jiou have been allowed to do as they please is because the royal family were huge wimps! Even that famine, for instance! It died down because some other town provided a huge pile of wheat for us! This is a chance to make up for the royal family's failings, and she should be grateful to have it!"

"Take that back, Merthophan!"

"Chrome! I've got something to say to you, too! You taking responsibility for the princess's disappearance? And letting yourself be reduced to running a cafeteria? How long are you gonna keep this up?!"

"None of your business…I've made my decision."

"I…I want you training our officer cadets. Come back to us! The war is close at hand!"

Merthophan was getting very worked up, as if steadfast in his resolve. Chrome just looked at him. "—You're drunk, Merthophan."

"I think you'd better quit while you're ahead," Choline added. "You're soberin' me right up...try not to think about war for a bit. You'll get yourself hurt, and I'll be the one who ends up cryin'."

This shut Merthophan's trap for good. He sat in silence for a long moment. Choline narrowed her eyes at him.

"If you're gonna puke, do it outside." She rubbed his back.

"...I'm okay, Choline. Sorry for yelling at you, Chrome."

Choline gave him a shoulder to lean on, and they vanished into the night, seeming to regret this whole thing. Chrome stared after them as something tugged at his heartstrings.

At the academy, mornings started early with endurance runs designed to build necessary stamina. No exceptions were made for mage or rear guards: Everyone followed the same routine.

"If you expect to protect the lives of others, you must be able to protect your own life by making yourself strong."

This was Merthophan's catchphrase, and all cadets had gone running every school day since the opening ceremony.

But on this day, their expressions were far less strained than usual.

"Whew...that was a good run," Riho exclaimed, finishing up amid a cloud of dust. "And today, all we've got is homeroom...and then, festival time! Three days of lyin' around and not doin' anything."

It was a half day. This was why everyone appeared in such good spirits.

Riho mopped up the sweat on her face with her shirt. She couldn't care less if her midriff was exposed. Beside her, Selen was using a towel to delicately wipe her brow. The difference in their upbringings was clear as day.

"*Sigh*...even if we don't have classes, we're still working security."

"Not all the time, though!" Riho grinned. "We're working in shifts, a few hours patrolling, then the rest is free time! It's practically a vacation!"

The foundation-day festival was almost here. Even though the cadets were working security, they'd have a lot of time to spare compared to their usual routine of training and classes. Along with Riho, most of their classmates were really looking forward to it.

With the morning training out of the way, the students hustled back to the classroom. In homeroom, the instructors covered the events of the festival in need of security, their patrol routes, and shifts. Then they were done for the day.

"Listen up, everyone," Merthophan announced, grimly, as if he was ready to give out a warning. "There will be foreign diplomats and leaders visiting our kingdom during the festival. And the number of tourists hits the yearly peak. You are not to allow any crimes to occur. Under no circumstances. Is that understood?"

His tone was as professional as ever, but there was extra gravitas to his little tirade. The relaxed smiles on the students' faces dissolved instantly. When he saw that, he nodded two, three times.

"Some of you were personally invited by me to take the admissions test to the academy—to prepare for a war that may someday arrive and to protect this land. Of course, there are those who were not, but it is my desire that all of you become soldiers...equally capable of protecting the realm. Bear that in mind on your patrols."

He was starting to monologue now. As if realizing he'd gotten carried away, he paused to clear his throat.

"*Ahem*... Excuse me. My point is, you are soldiers of the realm. Take pride in your position as you go about your duties. On your desks, you'll find the armbands that you'll be wearing on duty, as well as the festival schedules and maps. Make sure you look them over."

Merthophan wasn't quite himself today. Riho leaned over, whispering in Selen's ear.

"Something up with him?"

"I don't think it's right to pry into his private affairs, Riho. More importantly, I've got to find a way to invite Lloyd to see the festival with me... First, I need to know his schedule and then compare it with ours..."

As Selen lapsed into full-on stalker mode, Riho shuddered.

"Geez. I think you should look up the definition for the word *privacy...*"

Merthophan noticed them talking. "Riho Flavin, now is not the time for idle chatter. Or are you trying to tell me you haven't run enough and need to burn off more energy?"

Riho made a face like she'd rather die than do more laps, hastily stringing together an answer. "No, I was simply comparing my shift schedule with Selen's. Right?"

She turned to the Belt Princess, hoping she would back her up, but Selen's inability to take a hint was worse than Riho had imagined.

"Maybe I should cause an incident and use the chaos to lure him into a secluded corner..."

"Are you plotting something, there?" Merthophan asked, cocking an eyebrow.

Riho clutched her head and let out a silent screech.

"Gimme a break, m'lady Selen... Even you ought to know when Colonel Merthophan's in a bad mood."

Riho slumped against her desk, completely exhausted, as she sent daggers at Selen through half-lidded eyes.

Meanwhile, Selen was off in a world of her own. "Oh no, Sir Lloyd! We mustn't!"

She'd lost it, for sure.

"...You're always like this. I was an idiot."

Selen paid no attention to Riho at all. "Oh, Sir Lloyd... Did you forget we ate lunch an hour ago?"

"Wait. Don't tell me you've imagined so far into the future that he's already senile in your delusions."

"It's not a delusion! It's a projection! If I simulate potential scenarios, I'll be better equipped to handle them!"

This approach seemed more suited for soccer than love, but she remained oblivious to the penalty card called on her very existence.

"In that case, you should have projected the consequence of pissing the gentle sir Merthophan off today! Man, I wonder why he's been so pissy..."

"That should be obvious," Allan interrupted. "You seriously don't know?"

"...Eavesdropping, huh? What a great hobby. You and me are gonna get along great, Allan."

"Oh, don't drag me down to your level, you gold-digging mercenary... And? You really don't know?"

His arrogance was starting to get on her nerves, so she sneered, "I assume you'll do us the honor of filling us in."

"The search for the missing princess isn't going well. With the foundation-day festival almost here, he obviously wants to find her as soon as possible! That's why he's in such a bad mood. He's got to find her—no matter what!"

"...Dude, you're so off base."

Merthophan had not done a great job of hiding how unenthused he was about the search for the princess. Riho hadn't forgotten it.

"Whoops, I don't have time to waste chatting with the likes of you. I've gotta head to town."

"Sounds like you're the one obsessed with finding this princess. All your talk about promotion—you're as much of a gold digger as I am."

"But my ambitions aren't driven by money. Anyway, I'm gonna wrap this whole thing up, so why don't you try acting like a girl for once and chat about all the festival food you're dying to eat or some shit." Allan straightened his collar and turned to leave.

"Sure," Riho called after him. "Just make sure *you* don't end up getting gobbled up by some monster."

".........*Ngh!*" Allan flinched but elected to keep walking.

"What the...? He's acting a little weird, too."

"I suppose we'd better start looking for the princess!" Selen announced, jumping to her feet.

Riho stopped her. "I think you'd better come up with a better plan to find the mastermind than searching blindly. Any ideas?"

"Don't worry. This time, I promise not to yank out any hairs."

"Yeah, I think that's an unspoken prerequisite…but either way, not a plan."

Riho shuddered at her partner in crime's violent streak. In any normal case, she would have immediately gotten rid of someone like Selen, but she was a key figure in her plans to ride Lloyd's coattails. It was important to hang in there, be respectful, and keep the conversation going. Like any service job.

"I get where you're coming from… But we don't know the lay of the land here. Running around willy-nilly won't get us any good intel. I mean, our seniors have already been searching for years."

"That's true… It'd be a waste of time for us to run around with no real leads," Selen agreed.

"So…I've heard about a witch named Marie who deals in all kinds of information. Once we're ready, I think it'd be worth going to see her as early as tomorrow. I'd certainly like to find the princess and rub it Allan's dumb face."

"That sounds good. Please, take me with you." Selen was on board.

Riho made a ring with two fingers—a hand sign asking for moola—as she flashed her teeth. "Okay! In return, you pay for the info."

No trace of guilt. Selen had to laugh. "Smart," she chuckled. "A real gold digger, loud and proud."

It was a warm afternoon on the East Side—a district known primarily for its vulgarity and obscenities. But at this hour, it was still relatively peaceful and quiet.

In fact, the main roads were every bit as bustling as the North Side. Other than the seedy backroads, the area was relatively safe, but between the alarming things for sale, the powerful grips of promoters, and the practice of charging for "free" samples…well, it was easy to get ripped off.

"…This place is busier than I expected…though some of these shops seem really fishy, for sure," Selen commented.

The streets were stuffed with everything from fortune-tellers to army surplus to mystery delicacies and bizarre goods. The Witch of the East Side kept a general store surrounded by that sort of thing in an old building at the top of a hill. With a barely-there sign and strewn medicine pots with unknown contents, it didn't appear to be a shop at all.

"It doesn't seem like this place has ever been open…," Selen added. "I'm amazed you found out they sell information."

"I only just got wind of it. I was poking my head around here and there, and an old acquaintance clued me in… Gonna be working this kingdom awhile, so it's important to get to know people, m'lady."

"Hmm… Guess you do your groundwork, even though mercenaries might not look the part."

"Kinda got to if you wanna live free… You could stand to learn from us, Selen. Same for those soldiers. The less enemies you make, the more people might lend you a helping hand. Consider the consequences. A little friendly advice from me to you."

At this, Selen wrapped her fingers tightly around the cursed belt at her waist. "…I've never thought about consequences before."

There was a grim note in her voice.

"Uh, sorry." Riho meant it. "Hold up. You still have that thing around? Are ya sure you want it with you?"

"Yes… This is the precious red string of fate linking me to Lloyd… Plus, it saved my life the other day."

"…That's definitely the most horrifying red string around. Like, that thing really has a sinister aura to it…"

Riho was about to step inside, sensing that Selen was on the verge of launching into another tirade about love, but…

"Looks like they're closed."

Indeed, below the low-key shop sign was an even more low-key announcement: CLOSED.

"But there's steam coming out that window… Someone's gotta be here, at least."

And whoever that was must be cooking. There was a savory smell wafting through the air.

"…We came all this way, and we're pressed for time. Let's see if we can at least talk to her," Selen suggested and immediately gave a few short raps on the door.

In response, they heard footsteps pattering toward them.

The hinges creaked as the door opened, and a surprisingly familiar face appeared in front of them.

"Sorry! Marie's out, so we're closed for the day...wait..."

""Huh?!""

Standing in the doorway of the witch's shop was Lloyd, blinking back at them. Selen and Riho were equally at a loss for words.

"Come on in! Take a seat."

Before the girls' minds had a chance to start working again, Lloyd had ushered them inside. He quickly cleared two chairs at a table covered in old books and headed for the kitchen to put a pot of tea on the stove.

Riho managed to recover first and drew in a deep breath.

"I sure didn't expect you to be living at a witch's shop, Lloyd... Geez, m'lady Selen. I know he's your boyfriend and all, but you should tell me these things! We're *friends*, after all. I'm not gonna steal him or eat him... And whew! These kinds of surprises are bad for the heart."

But when Riho huffily turned to look at her...

"...Not in my wildest dreams! Lloyd and a witch? Not in my wildest dreams! Living together! Not in my...!"

Selen's expression betrayed whose heart this had affected most. And not just the heart. It was like her world had ended, or like she'd gone to drain her *yakisoba* noodles and accidentally dumped them in the sink.

"........."

Riho was beginning to have second thoughts about her read on the situation—and her failure to confirm it. For all Selen's talk about destiny and a fateful connection between them, she really didn't seem to know a thing about Lloyd.

"Uh, Selen...," Riho started, afraid to even ask. "Just to be sure... did you not know Lloyd was here?"

"—Erp." Selen's answer was more of a squeak.

"Er, is it true you and Lloyd are an item?"

"—Of course! It's mutual! Destiny! Like our fates have been tangled together by the red string of fate and then welded to an extra support pillar!"

What in the seismic retrofit...? Riho thought, but she elected not to say this out loud. Like a seasoned detective or a licensed therapist, she stuck to her guns, calmly asking the next question.

"Are you sure this isn't just all in your head? Is Sir Lloyd unaware of this?"

"That can't be true! How could I forget?! It was but a month ago!"

"NOPE! No need for your delusional ramblings, ma'am! Just answer the question, please."

"Listen! When I first met Lloyd—"

"Seriously, I don't... Wait, when you *first* met?"

"Yes! We first met a whole month ago. At the time—"

The admissions test had been about a month ago, which meant... Riho basically already had her answer.

They barely know each other!

Riho clutched her head at the fact that Selen was still doggedly referring to this as a mutual affair. Her mechanical arm made a loud clunk as it dug into her temples, but she was past the point of caring.

It's all starting to make sense! I bet Lloyd's ridiculous power freed her from the curse or something; and she decided she was destined to be with Lloyd, like a baby bird imprinting at first sight; and now here we are! Getting close to m'lady Selen so I could use Lloyd was a total waste of time!

At the center of this turmoil was Lloyd, who'd finished making the tea. He set their cups down carefully, making sure not to spill anything on the table.

"Sorry, Marie's out today...," he repeated. "Was there something you wanted?"

"This 'Marie' lady's life—," Selen hissed, the light fading from her eyes.

Riho stopped her just in the nick of time. "Don't, or you'll just make things worse. Uh, Lloyd…um, sir," she added quickly. "We were hoping to get some information."

Now that Riho knew Selen and Lloyd were basically strangers, there was no guarantee she'd survive any conflict against this monster, so her tone became much more deferential.

But Selen brushed her off, closing the distance to Lloyd. He tensed up.

"Yo… You're braver than the troops," Riho muttered.

Selen appeared to be equally oblivious to Riho's words and Lloyd's response.

"Sir Lloyd! Do you still want to join the academy?"

"Uh, yes. I didn't manage it this year, but next year…"

Selen stepped in even closer. "An exclusive offer—just for you! Your darling Selen has come running to bring you glad tidings!"

"G-glad tidings?"

Selen was so close that he could feel her breath on him. She took his hand, almost pressing herself against him.

"Yes! Are you aware that someone resembling the missing princess has been sighted in town?"

"Uh, yeah. I've heard the rumors."

She was so close that it was both physically and mentally difficult to converse with her. Riho decided to jump in before he got annoyed and unleashed his wrath, basically peeling Selen off him, but who cared? It was better than seeing her pounded flat.

"Mind telling us more, Lloyd…sir?" Riho tacked on for good measure, again in that uncharacteristically respectful voice.

"Unfortunately, I haven't heard anything more specific than that… Sorry."

He looked so apologetic, Riho hastily spluttered back a response. "Oh, no need to apologize! You've done nothing wrong! I assure you!"

"Uh, right… And uh, you don't need to be so deferential, Riho. I'm guessing we're almost the same age."

"I'm so sorry! Uh, I mean, my bad. Lloyd! Spare my life!"

This bizarre apology/display of forced familiarity elicited a gentle smile from Lloyd.

Now it was Selen's turn to cut in. "According to rumors, our people want to get her to safety before an enemy country gets their hands on her and uses her for political gain or executes her at the hands of the monsters. If we play our cards right, we might be able to get you enrolled as a reward for finding her."

"I see… That way, even someone as weak as me would have a chance to be a soldier."

What is he talking about? Riho wondered, staring at him with her sharp eyes. *He's still insisting that he's weak, after all this? Is this a trick to make us let our guard down? He's really dedicated to the bit.*

In her mind, this dedication (LOL) was just another reason to fear him.

"So, Lloyd… You've already defeated a bunch of monsters, right?"

"Ah-ha-ha, that's a good one. I've never even encountered any of them, much less defeated them! Uh, but there definitely are a lot of bugs crawling around these days. I guess because it's getting warmer? I keep seeing these twelve-foot-long locusts. Whenever I try to drive them off, they turn into ash."

Those are monsteeeers!

Riho turned to Selen, giving her a look that begged her to say something.

But Selen just smiled. "There are all sorts of weird bugs in the city!"

They're monsters, and you know it! Say something, goddammit!

If Lloyd said a color was black, Selen would readily agree—even if it was actually white, red, gold, or gray. Riho turned her glare from one to the other, screaming internally.

"I mean, monsters are much bigger," Lloyd continued. "They're like three-story buildings! You'd know right away. And they usually have second and third forms…"

Riho clutched her aching stomach, afraid to hear any more. "F-fine, they're just locusts… Yay, locusts. Locusts forever," she yielded.

Meanwhile, Selen stared at Lloyd with the glittering eyes of a maiden in love. "That settles it! We should immediately head to a nearby inn to deepen our relationship! And then you should enlist and be my roommate!"

"Slow down there! In so many ways! My stomach can't handle this!"

If Riho let Selen babble on, she could very well propose that they share a grave together. On the other hand, Lloyd thought monsters were mere insects... Clutching her stomach, she pondered this new information as she tried to deal with an extraordinary human and a stupid one.

He's the one who drove off the locusts, huh...? And as if that wasn't terrifying enough, he doesn't even know monsters are monsters... Oh god, now my head's pounding, too.

When Lloyd noticed Riho rubbing her stomach, he took something off the shelf and handed it to her.

"Oh, take this."

"What could this...I mean, what the heck is this?"

A powder wrapped in wax paper, carrying a medicinal scent. Riho shot Lloyd a look when she realized this must be for her upset stomach.

"...You sure? I can have this?"

"Of course!" That same gentle smile. "We're friends, aren't we?"

"...Come again? Friends? Seriously? Us?"

Riho looked askance at this. She was a mercenary, after all, which meant relationships were all contingent on a reciprocal exchange. She'd accepted gifts in return for a favor later, but she'd never once been given anything for free. And given that they'd only met once during the admissions test...well, this gave her a lot to consider.

If he's saying we're friends, that means he thinks I'll be useful to him... but how? I'm no match for him in combat...which leaves me with...my body. Could he be after that?

Since her definition of friendship required an equal exchange, she had to consider what he might want in return.

But I'm a scrawny, beady-eyed, one-armed...no, wait! Now that I think about it, he's the one who approached me first, tellin' me my arm was cool and all that... Maybe that's his kink? Or my small boobs?

Riho shot Lloyd a searching glance. From his perspective, Riho had just gone still, not making a move to touch the medicine at all. He was looking increasingly worried.

…*Oh god, he's starting to look like the kinda guy who* would *be into the tiniest of chests…*

(Please submit a detailed report on what these people look like. For research purposes, obviously.)

At any rate, his open and honest smile had started to look like anything but—which makes sense, since people in stressful situations often lose their capacity for rational thought.

I never thought this bony body would actually be my saving grace! For the first time I'm grateful for my genes! A big thank-you to my parents! And thank you, god of small boobs!

Her train of thought had rapidly moved on to idolatry. (Please see the note about people under pressure above.)

But as Riho started to pray to an extremely problematic religion—likely to inspire some weirdly devout followers, no doubt—Lloyd was looking at her with concern all over his itty-bitty-titty-loving face (LOL).

"A-are you sure you're okay?"

"Uh, yeah, I'm fine. I was just giving thanks to my parents and the god of small boobs. Not that I've ever met either."

Lloyd blinked at the baffling mention of this unfamiliar deity but decided to ask about the other thing instead.

"Sma— Er, no, you've never met your parents?"

"Yeah, I'm an orphan," she mentioned, like it was no big deal.

"I—I see. Sorry." He bowed his head in apology. "Didn't mean to pry."

"Oh, don't worry about it. I'm, like, way over it. Just tryin' to live one day at a time."

Lloyd seemed extremely relieved by this. "That's good…but now I know why I had this feeling about you, Riho. Like a sort of empathy thing?"

"Huh?" This last turn of phrase confused her.

"Oh, I don't have parents, either," Lloyd admitted bashfully. "Same as you. I was taken in by the people in my village and raised by them."

"…Oh. I see."

He didn't seem to be lying, but she didn't really know how to take this, so she settled for scratching her head.

And then she got mad at herself.

No, no, no, don't let him fool you, Riho Flavin! A con artist's first trick is to make their target identify with them! Did you forget what happens when you trust people willy-nilly?

Phantom pain shot through her arm—a sharp tinge from the tips of fingers long since replaced with machinery.

Think this through: That diabolically innocent smile, that sincere tone of voice, that petite body that you just want to snuggle against, like a small animal! Oh, and that cute way he said we were friends, trying to get all up close and personal with me! It's all a trick to make me let my guard down! And the biggest red flag is this face of his—he clearly likes small boobs!

Now that she'd thoroughly psyched herself out, Riho chose her words carefully, knowing that refusing the medicine entirely could have terrifying consequences. She was forced to accept it.

"Thanks! Seriously, thanks. I'll make sure to take it. Get this coated all over my insides!"

She accepted the medicine with both hands, bending at the waist like she was accepting a diploma. Lloyd read this wrong.

"You needed the medicine that bad? Then take more! It's all hand-made by Marie and super effective. There's more in back!"

He dashed off into the back room.

Riho collapsed in a chair, sweating like a boxer who'd just finished twelve rounds.

…Goddamn…I really wanna get a good look at the information broker who lives with this monster. No, we just gotta get some info and then book it outta here to get Lloyd enlisted—so that he owes me one. Or should I let sleeping dogs lie and use the info for myself?

Riho was hitting the brakes on all her plans, reconsidering her course of action as she waited for the person in question to arrive to the scene.

*   *   *

It wasn't long before Marie returned, as if back by popular demand. Long black robes, pointy hat, and an expensive brooch that added to the whole vibe—one glance at her and it was clear she was a witch.

But the first thing that left her mouth made her seem less like a witch and more like a businesswoman who'd just gotten off work.

"Argh, what a waste! Came up empty again. We've all got our good days and bad days, I guess. Whatever, I've got a homemade meal by Lloyd waiting for me! I'll cast an ice spell to make this ale nice and cold and... Ahhh, ale in the middle of the day! Being a witch is the best—huh?"

...Okay, maybe more like a middle-aged man. But as she stepped cheerily into the shop, she found two strange guests sitting there waiting for her, even though the shop was clearly closed. She looked at them, bug-eyed.

In the back was a slender woman with beady eyes, the front of her jacket all the way open in a seductive way. She bobbed her head in greeting.

But that wasn't the problem: It was the beautiful blond woman sitting in front of her.

"*Sorry to intrude*," muttered the blond—Selen—in a strained voice. There was an audible creak as she forced the corners of her mouth into a grin, but her eyes weren't smiling at all. They seemed possessed of a dark void.

"Er, uh...sure..."

The infinite darkness radiating off this girl was enough to make Marie feel uncomfortable in her own home.

"Well, don't just stand there. *Go ahead, sit down!*" Selen waved Marie to a seat.

(Whose house was this again?)

"Oh, sorry." In a state of complete befuddlement, Marie moved toward the chair.

Creeeeeeeeaaak.........

*   *   *

Selen's head rotated, making an audible noise as she traced Marie's movements.

Marie let out a little shriek. *Huh? What did I do? She's got me in her sights!*

She'd found herself in mortal danger for reasons unbeknownst to her, and Marie tried to convince herself she was imagining it. To test out her new theory, she rocked herself from right to left.

Swshhhh.
Creeeak.

Selen's head moved in perfect synchrony.

…Oh, come on! I haven't done anything to deserve this! There must be some mistake! She just so happened to move her head from side to side when I moved!

Marie rocked herself faster, leaning even farther, in a desperate attempt to prove it was just a coincidence.

Shpp, shpp, shpp, shpp, shpp.

"What are you doing? Please, sit down."

"Oh, right."

Marie stopped her bizarre movements and hastily took a seat, like a student scolded for goofing off in class. She wiped her sweating hands on her robe, feeling very uncomfortable.

"Oh, Marie! You're back!"

At last, a familiar figure stepped into the room. Lloyd.

"Lloyd! I—I just got back."

After feeling like a stranger in her own crib for quite some time, Marie was so relieved to see the boy that she got up and started to run over to him.

"Sit! Down!"

"Eep! Okay."

Inexplicably, the dark aura seeping out of the blond had somehow gotten even deeper. Marie snapped back into her chair in fear.

As if he'd sensed the awkward tension in the room, Lloyd introduced the two of them. "Oh, these are friends of mine. Riho and Selen."

"'Sup. I'm Riho." Riho bobbed her head again. With a sweeping look up and down, she was clearly appraising Marie…but Marie's attention was fully on the other one.

"*Pleasure!* I'm his 'friend,' Selen," she spat dryly. Her gaze was too shrouded in darkness to tell what she was thinking.

"H-hello, I'm Marie. They call me the Witch of the East Side."

"I see. Marie, huh? What a *killer* name."

"Thanks, Selen."

"And they call you the Witch of the East Side? *Slay.*"

"—Um, I swear your compliments are just the teeniest bit homicidal…"

Selen's lips twisted. "Must be your imagination…"

"Oh, good…I hoped it was."

"And when do the witch trials begin?"

I'm not imagining it! She made it absolutely clear! She's here to kill me! Why? For what? Does day drinking grate on her moral code?!

As Marie's confusion reached its peak, Riho decided they were getting nowhere and cut in by restraining Selen.

"Okay, okay, that's enough, Selen. So, witch lady. Thing is, we've been asked to find someone by our superiors, and we're hoping to buy some information from you."

This helped Marie calm down a little.

Superiors? Information? Come to think of it…

Marie had been a wee bit too preoccupied by Selen to realize it, but when she gave Riho a once-over, she recognized her uniform as one of an officer cadet—and the girl was sporting a metal arm so ginormous it was a wonder she'd failed to notice it until now.

"The mercenary, Riho Flavin…and are you the Belt Princess, Selen Hemein?"

"Oh? You know who we are?"

"You don't have to be an information dealer to know that much. You're two of the cadets that Colonel Merthophan personally recruited."

"If you know that, then I guess you're in the right business."

As Marie spoke to Riho, her manncrisms slowly assumed those of a witch once more, activating her exaggerated speech patterns.

"I certainly have my reservations about you two, but if you're here as customers, that's another story. Especially if you're friends with Lloyd… Fine! I've finished my errands, so I'll open up shop for you. Allow me to guide your paths."

"Nice! Lucky us!" Riho exclaimed with a grin.

"However," Marie started, launching into her usual spiel. "According to tradition, witches have demanded equal payment in return for granting your desires. If you choose not to heed to my warning and desire information…just make sure you don't regret it."

"Oh, you're speakin' my language. Yeah, the juicer the gossip, the more expensive the price. According to tradition. You know your stuff."

"Oh, mm."

Riho had taken a witch's threat as flavor text from a skilled haggler, but she'd also dropped a compliment, so Marie let it slide for now.

Riho yanked a photograph out of her shirt pocket. It showed a young princess…in other words, it was a picture of Marie herself at age ten.

"We're looking for her."

"…………" All expression drained from Marie's face—a total absence of any emotion.

"Uh…hey, witch lady?"

"We're closed today," she announced, getting up to leave.

"Wait!" Riho shouted. "What happened to that big dramatic speech?!"

"T-today, er…I just don't have anything good! So shop's closed until I find something worth spreading! Yeah. Not feeling it!"

She was starting to sound like a stubborn owner of a ramen shop, making excuses like, "The soup don't taste quite right, so we ain't open." Marie had completely forgotten to act like a witch.

And once she'd spluttered this very obvious lie, she figured everything out.

I get it! That's why this Selen girl was scowling at me! She knows who I am! And the royals are so hell-bent on starting a war, and they've got her riled up to a murderous rage! That must be it! Our land is in peril, and here I was, thinking about quaffing ale in the afternoon! Why wouldn't she be pissed?!

It goes without saying that Selen's headspace contained absolutely no room for politics, crammed to the absolute brim with sweet Lloyd-related fantasies like red-bean paste in a pastry.

Marie was in a panic, heedless of the baffled look on Riho's face.

I can't let myself get caught right before the foundation-day festival... right before D-Day! I still don't know who's behind this! But if I'm caught now...

"Your pathetic little excuse isn't gonna cut...uh, Marie?"

Marie was still panicking, oblivious to Riho's voice.

I've got to worm my way out of this! Don't lose hope! You can do it! You put up with that loli *grandma for years! This is nothing compared to that!*

"Helloooooooo? Anyone home? Why are you clutching your head, witch lady?"

"Don't worry. Hope is not yet lost."

"Hope...? Whatever. Just tell us if you've got any intel or not."

Marie adjusted her glasses, doing her best to appear calm. "Unfortunately, I have no information on the missing princess."

"...No one said it was the princess."

All hopes were dashed.

Marie smacked her head on the table.

"Hmm," Riho murmured, as if realizing something.

Selen cut in. "Riho, listen. She says she doesn't know. That's that."

"Hey! M'lady! ...You can't just—"

As her teeth ground together, Selen's eyes bored holes in Marie's skull, looking ready to let out some tears of blood.

"Plus, I'm far more interested in Marie herself! Your day-to-day routine, your family life...*I want to hear it right from your lips.*"

She knows! She knows I'm the princess! Why else would she ask that?!

This inky aura forced Marie to sit bolt upright. She managed to work up enough nerve to knead her hands together, trying to cover her tracks.

"U-um, I'm just a normal witch from the East Side! Nothing more, nothing less."

"Then why did your voice go all squeaky? Are you hiding something from us? Or..." Riho smirked. "Are you the princess yourself?"

At this, Lloyd leaned in, looking at the photo.

"Hmm." He smiled. "It does look a little like you...but this is the princess, right?"

"Uh, yeah. The missing princess."

Lloyd took another long look at it, but it didn't seem to add up for him. "I guess I can see the resemblance," he offered. "But I don't think Marie is any kind of princess."

"What are you trying to say, Lloyd? Am I not classy enough? Rude," Marie quipped, beaming and sticking two thumbs up.

"Your face and words don't match up," Riho said.

"Hee-hee-hee. I mean, just the other day, you were so drunk that you thought the sink was the bath. And you started taking your robe off right here. Plus, every time the village chief shows up, you end up on your hands and knees begging for mercy or spraying coffee out your nostrils... You won't believe how much work it is wiping her face, cleaning up after her, doing her laundry! No way she's a princess."

"Y-yeah, I'm no princess..."

"She says with tears in her eyes," narrated Riho.

His anecdotes didn't stop at challenging her identity as a princess, steamrolling over her identity as a woman.

"............"

As Lloyd talked, Selen became gloomier. Imagine hearing your special someone brag on and on about their romantic escapades with their current lover.

"You seem to be really enjoying yourselves. How many years have you been living here (*together*)?!" Selen shrieked.

To Marie's ears, this sounded a lot like, "How many years have you been shirking your royal duties?"

She answered apologetically. "T-two years."

"Two years! Two! Years! Two years of living the life (*as newlyweds*)?!"

Tears started welling out of the twin voids on Selen's face as she fled to the kitchen, unable to bear it any longer. Marie found such grief intolerable.

Yes...I've been away five years and lived here for two. Any normal citizen would wonder why I'm living large when the royal family is pushing for war... Of course, she'd spite me for it. She must be a real patriot.

In truth, Selen couldn't care less about royal affairs—so long as it didn't concern Lloyd. She'd fret more about a waitress serving her the wrong thing at a diner than about a princess disappearing.

Meanwhile, Riho was observing things closely, aware that the two weren't on the same page. While Selen was washing her face in the kitchen, Riho asked Marie a question, quietly enough to not be overheard.

"So how long has Lloyd been staying with you?"

"Uh, just before the admissions test...like a month?"

"That's what I figured... Anything between you two?"

"He's like a nephew? ...Or like my master's grandson?"

"Nephew... Thanks."

That was all Riho needed. Lloyd clearly didn't know anything about Marie at all. Just as this conversation concluded, Selen rejoined them with puffy eyes.

"I hate you so much... But I want to hear the truth directly from you... Answer me honestly."

With palpable resolve in Selen's voice, Marie decided she'd better admit the truth herself.

It's my duty to respond to my people… If I tell her the truth, maybe I can convince her to keep quiet a few more days.

"*Yum.* This tea. *Delicious.*" Riho was hoping this farce would wrap itself up soon.

Lloyd was just fidgeting awkwardly, unsure what to do.

"All right. I'll answer honestly. No more lies." Marie spoke with a new tranquility that made Selen clench her hands over her heart.

"You're—"

"Yes. I'm—"

"—Lloyd's wife, right?"

"The prin—his *what*?!"

An awkward silence settled over the room. All they could hear was the hustle and bustle of the street outside.

"Um, Selen…? I have no idea what you're talking about."

"I can't believe you'd play innocent now, you thief! You said you'd tell me the truth! This is your last chance to beg forgiveness! And you, Sir Lloyd! This is your last chance to take advantage of me!"

With that last bit, Selen quickly started to unbutton her shirt, throwing caution to the wind.

"You're getting a bit carried away, Selen!" Riho yelped, foiling her efforts at her home-wrecking striptease (LOL).

Lloyd looked completely baffled the whole time. "Huh? Take advantage? What?"

"Pretend you didn't hear that last part! It's nothing!"

"You're sure? Oh, I know! I'll make a new pot of tea."

Lloyd headed to the kitchen, sensing this clearly wasn't ending any time soon—just like a perceptive housewife quietly leaving a husband to his important discussions.

Riho watched him go and then started talking Selen down. She was getting good at this.

"Listen, Selen. This lady is like his relative."

"What?! But relatives shouldn't—"

"No, no, yeesh, not like that. You know how when people first move to the city, they stay with distant relatives, right?"

"But for two years?"

"Marie's lived here for two years. Lloyd's only been here a month!"

"But! That just means they've had over thirty chances! No way nothing happened!"

"Chances for *what*?!"

"Then why didn't she tell me that when she introduced herself? She should have led by insisting she didn't take advantage of him!"

"Who would do that?! You didn't introduce yourself by saying, 'I'm Selen, and I've yet to get to first base with Sir Lloyd,' did you?!"

This last howl finally got through to Selen.

"Well," she replied, much calmer. "You're right. I would only introduce myself as, 'I'm Selen, and I've got to first base with Sir Lloyd,' after the fact."

"Sure. Though that intro would definitely strike out in all social circles."

A natural sparkle returned to Selen's eyes as she turned to Marie and apologized to the best of her ability.

"I'm so sorry for this misunderstanding."

"Oh, not at all...I'm sorry, too. He's basically like a nephew to me."

They both smiled and chuckled after making up. Riho laughed, too, a malicious smirk playing on her lips. She put a hand on Marie's shoulder, waving the photo around.

"So, back on topic...you know this girl?"

"………"

Riho had let Marie dig her own hole, which Marie had jumped right into, gladly. Her loss was clear.

"You got all the way to *prin* earlier. Just one more syllable to go!"

"...Please, at least give us a clue," Selen begged. The look in her eyes was so serious (and devoid of darkness) that Marie reconsidered.

"I know you have to answer to your superiors, but why are you so desperate to find her? Would you mind giving me some insight?"

"If we find her, we can get Sir Lloyd enlisted in military school."

Marie turned to Riho, who nodded in agreement.

"You're not lying… Well, he's certainly got some good friends."

"Obviously, I have no intention of remaining *just* friends."

This gave Marie even more food for thought, but before she could say anything else…

"Excuse me! Is the witch here?"

Two arrogant delinquents burst into the shop without even bothering to knock. Their shoulders and hands were wrapped in bandages as if they'd fallen down and hurt themselves.

It was the same pair who'd tried to mug Lloyd—and gotten what they deserved, although Lloyd himself had no idea he was responsible for their injuries.

Marie frowned at them. "You…don't seem like you're here to buy potions."

"What didja say? Hey, look at that! You're here after all! Geez, take that closed sign down if you're open!"

"They aren't buying potions, Marie," Riho called out, making sure the delinquents could hear. "Not unless you got potions that can cure stupid."

This sneer clearly infuriated the two, but the younger one stopped his boss from doing anything.

"Boss, Boss! That's, you know, the infamous mercenary chick, Riho! She's bad news."

"Yeah? So what?"

"And the girl next to her is…the Cursed Belt Princess. The one who's been wandering the North and South Sides, lookin' for someone—and rumored to yank out body hair."

"Yeah? So what?! That's kind of a turn-on!"

"Me too, Boss! She's bad in a good way!"

"See, m'lady Selen? Normal people don't rip out hair during interrogations. Or you might get men like them."

"Lesson learned."

*   *   *

All parts of this conversation were equally flustering to Marie, but the delinquents didn't seem to care.

"Anyway, we're here for info!" He took a photograph out of his pocket.

""""What?!""""

All three shouted at once. After all, it was the same photo in Riho's hands.

When he saw her photo, he figured it all out.

"Huh, you were hired to find this princess by that guy, too? Great! Tell us everything you know!" he threatened.

Once again, the younger one tried to talk some sense into his hotheaded partner. "Boss! That's insane! We're still in recovery!"

"You dumbass," he scolded. "What are you afraid of? We've fought someone way scarier and lived to tell the tale! Don't tell me you forgot already?!"

"How could I?!"

"Yeah, that was the worst. The most terrifying person in the world. He thought nothing of maiming us. I'll never forget the look on his face! It went right past terror, straight into mystifying! I didn't even understand my own feelings!"

"And my shoulder went right past a natural angle…"

"But we survived! We're both! Still alive! There is nothing left to fear!"

Marie watched the two get amped up, feeling like she was watching a mini-play by a local theater troupe.

When they finally finished and faced the three girls, they were ready to fight.

Each had taken out a knife, edging closer with a menacing scowl.

"Point is, we ain't scared of anything but *that one kid*! Spit it out, loud and clear! Make sure we understand every word!"

"You heard him! Tell us everything you know! And answer all the questions we didn't ask!"

As if summoned by their theatrics, "that one kid" appeared from the kitchen with a fresh pot of tea.

"Oh, more customers?"

Thud.

Both foreheads hit the ground as the two groveled before him.

Everyone was sipping tea, gazing at the delinquents as they sat on their heels with stick-straight spines in the corner, playing the part of the world's most tasteless statues.

"So," Riho called out. "Why the hell are you out looking for the princess? And who is this 'guy' that hired you?"

"We received! Orders from! A man who kept his face hidden!" the older one shouted, making sure to enunciate each word.

"He didn't care how! Just said to bring her to him! Dead or alive!" the younger one added, unprompted.

This alarming news got a reaction from Selen. "...Dead?"

"Yes! He said it! And that's not all!"

"We heard him! Right after we accepted the job! He was talking to himself!"

At this point, they were blabbing their mouths off and started reenacting the scene.

"'If the princess returns now, it'll ruin everything. I must do everything I can to prevent it...'"

Marie's eyes narrowed. She got off her chair and moved closer, pressing them. "Did he say anything else? Did you recognize him? Tell me everything you can remember!"

"Well...there was something he kept muttering under his breath."

The two delinquents counted down together. "''Three, two, one... 'For the peace of the realm.'''"

"...Is that...?"

Riho and Selen glanced at each other. Marie gestured for the criminals to leave, and they bowed their heads repeatedly as they exited. Once they were finally gone, the witch turned to the cadets.

"You have a hunch about who might have hired them to kill the princess?"

"Well, yeah...but we've been hired to protect her. Killing her is a totally different story." Riho couldn't hide a note of panic.

Selen seemed to feel the same way.

Marie put her hand to her chin, trying to process this. "I'm guessing it's the exact same person trying to start this war," she muttered under her breath. "They're giving orders to kill the princess to prevent her from joining the anti-war faction—while they still have control of the king. War or no war, the situation is clearly at its breaking point... which might be just the chance I need."

A stream of ominous words. The others were all staring at her.

"The anti-war faction? I'm so lost..."

"Sorry, but can you tell me who you suspect? I need that name."

Marie's determination definitely got to Riho, but she took a few steps closer, doing her best to stand her ground.

"Geez...you want a favor from me, you oughtta make your identity clear."

"I think you already know, Mercenary...you know who I am."

They glared at each other like boxers in a ring.

Then a timid voice cut through the tension, seeming entirely out of place.

Lloyd had finally broken his silence.

"Sorry, Marie. I think I've figured out who you are, too."

"Lloyd?"

"I've been wondering for a while...but I was never quite sure. Marie, you're—"

Marie shuddered. He was clearly unsure if he should be saying this at all.

...Does he really know I'm the princess?

The photo. All that talk of people searching for the princess. Ongoing discussions of impending war. If he put all those facts together, he might well be onto her. But she couldn't bring herself to admit it.

The reason was simple: She wanted to keep things the way they were… If he knew her true identity, Lloyd would almost certainly change the way he treated her. And that would be unbearable.

"……Uh, Lloyd."

Even if there was an obvious difference in rank, she wanted him to interact with her in the same way. She was about to say that—

"You're this country's hero…Marie the Savior."

"Who in the hell is that?!"

—but his cryptic conclusion defied all expectations.

Marie could only gape at him, completely flabbergasted, to which Lloyd replied, "Don't deny it!" and proceeded to demonstrate the deductive reasoning that closed this case.

"There's no need to hide the truth. The carpenter called you the Savior of the East Side…"

Oh, that damn carpenter and his big mouth! You made everything that much more complicated!

She could imagine the old man sipping tea and grinning at her even as she swore at him.

"That's not all. Every time I go shopping, I hear stories about someone fighting for the sake of this kingdom from the shadows."

That "someone" is you.

Marie stared at the oblivious boy in disbelief, struggling to keep her eyes open. After all, she'd heard from Lloyd himself about how he'd used his superhuman strength to fix a dried-up river or clean up the blocked road. But he tromped on with his off-target logic.

"I knew for sure when I heard about the monsters. It seems like I've been hearing about someone defeating them everywhere I go. I was never attacked myself and never caught a glimpse of any of them, but I know now that's because Marie was moving ahead of me, taking out all the monsters for me."

Nope, that was all you.

Of course, these rumors had spread because he'd exterminated them like insects wherever he went.

As his speech came to a close, Lloyd adjusted his posture, bowing his head to her. "Please, Marie! I want to pay you back for everything you've done. I'll do anything I can!"

Marie clutched her head. Out of the corner of her eye, she'd seen Selen's nose start bleeding the moment Lloyd said *anything.* Marie wanted to give him a big hug and whisper, "Thank you," but she was hesitant to act. She was afraid of Alka turning her into a frog, and...

If I let him help, she'll take Lloyd home. Then his dream will never come true... No, that's not it.

She closed her eyes, sighing, before she let herself be completely honest.

I just want to be with him... Huh.

That's right. The real reason she couldn't drag him into this mess was because it meant he'd leave her side. They'd only been living together a month, but that had been more than enough.

How can I explain this so he'll accept it? I'd have to first convince him that he's impossibly strong, then explain that the loli *grandma will be furious if I dipped into that strength... Is that something I can pull off before the end of the day?*

When she realized that it'd be a tough road ahead of her, Marie went with a much more desperate plan.

"Now that you've figured out my true identity, I don't need to hide it any longer. I'm the talk of the town, the knight of this country—Marie the Hero," she proclaimed.

She'd abandoned all hope of explaining things to Lloyd and decided to wholeheartedly embrace his misunderstanding.

"And as the town's savior...I'm afraid you're just too weak to help," she concluded by beating around the bush.

Lloyd became more earnest. "I know I'm weak. But I want to be one of those cool soldiers, and they'd never stand idly after hearing this! I don't know what I can do, but...!"

Marie winced, knowing they could easily solve everything and then some if they joined forces. Lloyd clearly wanted to help, and his earnest gaze seemed to pierce straight into her chest. Not because he was literally staring at her tits or anything, just…you know, *metaphorically.*

But even as Marie hated herself for it, she met his sincere stare head-on, adopting the role of the savior. "I'm glad you feel that way, but you mustn't follow me… You're just not strong enough. Heed the warning of the Savior of the East Side."

"But…I couldn't possibly bear to not do anything after hearing this…I know! I know better than anyone I'll be useless! But still—"

You don't get it at all! You'd be crazy useful, you knucklehead!

She was getting frustrated, but she elected to redirect that energy and gave him a fierce glare.

But Lloyd met her gaze, undeterred, with a determined look in his eyes.

"You've helped me out so much since I got here, Marie! I owe you! I don't want to be the kind of man who can't help important people in my life when they're in trouble!"

What are you saying? …You're the one who's helped me!

For years, Marie had been in hiding, waiting for her chance to get her father back, and Lloyd had reminded her of the comforting warmth of a family, acting like a little brother to her.

And he'd handled all the cooking, cleaning, laundry, and finances, so…

Oh god! He's my gigolo!

Her wallet and stomach belonged to him now. Marie buried her face in her hands. Lloyd definitely read that gesture wrong, because he got even more worked up.

"I'll do anything! I can't bear the idea of doing nothing…"

Once again, he'd brandished the world's most legendary weapon: "I'll do anything."

Marie snapped, finally losing her temper. "You think you can say that without any consequences? You'll do anything? You'll try your best? You think saying that will get you what you want? If you keep it up, you'll have a whole slew of horrible people taking advantage of you!"

*   *   *

Selen: "I'm not horrible, so I can take advantage of him, right?"
Riho: "Yeah, the only thing horrible about you is that brain of yours."

Marie gritted her teeth, spitting out her words.
But her anger wasn't directed at Lloyd.
This is awful.
She was mad at herself. Lloyd was hesitant by nature, but here he was, being assertive at last, and she was forced to nip his progress in the bud.
"...I...," he started.
"You coming would be a liability..."
The pain of speaking against what she really wanted must have made her sound extra harsh, because he flinched and then hung his head, trailing off toward the door.
"Lloyd?" Selen called after him, but he didn't look up.
Dragging his feet, he trudged over to the shop door. "Sorry," he muttered. "I need to cool my head. I'm...really sorry."
His usual gentle demeanor clouded over. With a hint of chilly gloom in his voice, Lloyd went outside. Even the sound of the door creaking shut seemed forlorn. Marie watched him go with a dismal expression and took a deep breath when he was gone.
"Look, sorry. But now that you've heard this much, I'm going to have to ask for your cooperation in eliminating those attempting to use the royal family to wage war."
Marie tugged her pointy hat off her head. Without it, she bore a striking resemblance to the girl in the photograph.
"Consider it a request direct from the princess of Azami—Maria Azami."
"You're...the princess?!" Selen stammered.
"Yeesh, you only just pieced that together, m'lady? Whatever." Riho narrowed her eyes, moving closer to Marie. "You finally being honest with us, Your Highness? But there's a lot that doesn't add up. And until I'm clear on that, I'm not helping anyone—royalty or not."

"That's fair. First, the anti-war faction and a group of—"

"Yada yada yada! I don't care about that! Why'd you refuse Lloyd's help? You know what I'm talking about! Lying to his face until he backed down? He was almost in tears! You live with him, don't ya? You've gotta know how strong he is!"

"That's right, Your Highness! Sir Lloyd would be a huge asset! How can you call yourself royalty after passing on his wonderful offer? He said he'd 'do anything'!"

"Uh, Selen, your anger seems misdirected...," Riho noted, giving her some major side-eye.

Marie chuckled. "You seem to have quite the reputation, but you're actually pretty sweet, huh?" she said. "...I'm glad you got angry on his behalf."

This hit the nail on the head, and Riho failed to find the words to protest it, grunting "*Ngh!*" with dramatic flair.

"There are a lot of reasons," Marie continued. "I'll walk you through them. First..."

With a dour look, she told the two cadets that Lloyd was from Kunlun. Their scowls quickly turned to looks of surprise, and those softened into expressions of understanding—it certainly explained everything about his bizarre abilities.

"In conclusion, if I let him get mixed up in this, I'll be turned into a frog."

"I don't see how that's a major problem. In fact, I see it as a benefit. You could live in the water and on land. Plus, you can choose whether to breathe with your lungs or skin. Come on, amphibians have it good, regardless of gender! Like six times better, if we're rounding. I think we're going to have to bring Sir Lloyd on board and spend the entire night exploring his definition of *anything*."

Selen was clearly more hung up on that one word than with his outlandish background, passionately delivering a presentation on the benefits of being a frog with the enthusiasm of a new employee leading a project meeting for the first time.

"Oh, and if we get caught, Lloyd'll get dragged back home, and we'll never see him again," Marie added.

"Now that I think about it, I've suddenly remembered seeing frogs stuck to my window in summer, which was super gross, which would obviously be a problem. Never mind!"

Selen immediately changed her tune with the haste of a new employee, afraid to contradict anyone at the office.

Riho had a lot to chew on. *If he was just a country kid, I could have done so much with him!*

"So he really doesn't have parents, then…and his kindness and the line about being friends—none of that was a trap or a performance."

He hadn't been lying about the "sort of empathy thing," either. Riho was oddly happy to learn the truth, not that Marie had any way of knowing this. Although she did wonder about the smile playing over Riho's lips, she elected to focus on the task at hand instead.

"And again, I'm sorry, but I could really use some help. If this gets out of hand, god only knows what'll happen. I want to handle it with a small, concentrated force."

"All righty, Your Highness."

"That was quick. Are you sure?"

"It's a chance to have royalty owe me a favor…but if I'm being honest, I'm feeling some empathy myself. I know how it feels to have to be the bad guy."

Selen agreed once she calmed down. "I'll help, too. As long as I'm a soldier, I'll do what I can—for the sake of the realm and for the peace of all."

"…Thank you."

"Plus! Once this is settled, you use your princess powers to get Sir Lloyd enlisted in the academy! Put him in my dorm, in the same room as me! Pretty please! And I demand you issue a Sir-Lloyd-will-do-anything ticket!"

Selen was definitely far more passionate about the latter half of her little spiel.

"…I'll do what I can," Marie replied vaguely in the way of a true politician.

This girl's frenzied devotion to Lloyd was starting to give Marie

major flashbacks—images of Alka pulsing through her head in a diz-
zying carousel. Marie shook this off and gave them both a serious look.

"Then let's get down to business... Let's resolve this without incident
so we can smile at him once more—"

No turning back now. The two cadets met her gaze with determination and nodded.

The evening sun had turned the shop in the East Side red. As the
two made their leave, Marie let the chair take the full weight of her
exhausted body. Between Chrome and the two cadets, she finally had
enough help, but the situation with Lloyd was really weighing her
down.

*Get your head straight, Maria. Focus on freeing your father from his
curse—without the mastermind stopping you. If they manage to block
me using runes, I'm in trouble; I can't exactly use them multiple times in
a row.*

In the corner of her mind, she thought, *But Lloyd could.* It would be
so much easier with his help—and she knew full well that wasn't the
only reason behind it. When she came to, she realized her hand was
clutching the brooch, a gift from him to her.

The sad look on his face was burned into the back of her mind, but
she attempted to shake it off, looking out the window at the sun setting
over the town.

*Yes, everything will be settled tomorrow. My father will be freed, and I
might be back to my old life...but...*

She sighed and let herself voice her fears.

"I might die...huh."

In light of this realization, even the view outside her window seemed
precious. She squinted at the filthy road outside, recounting the day
when she first opened her shop and looking out at her gruff but kind
neighbors, and Alka, soaking wet—

"Wait, why are *you* here and why are you wet?!" Marie yelped, spotting a surprising figure outside her window.

Alka staggered forward, entering through the front door and, dripping with water, plopped down on a chair with a heavy plunk. She turned toward Marie with a squelching sound.

"...I heard everything. I reckon ya managed to keep your promise 'bout not getting me and Lloyd mixed up in this mess."

Marie looked apologetic, assuming Alka had used some arcane art to eavesdrop on their earlier conversation. "I hope I didn't worry you too much. I'll do my best to solve this problem on my own..."

"Darn tootin'. You really stood your ground. If the villagers got mixed up in human affairs, I reckon it would never end and be a real pain in the—I mean, prevent y'all from personal growth."

Even though the chief almost slipped up and revealed her true thoughts, Marie let it pass, hanging her head.

"I appreciate that," she responded with admiration. "This is my problem, and I should solve it with my own hands."

"*Hngg*, this is really throwin' me off my A game," Alka grumbled, looking disgruntled. "If this situation right here involved a demon lord or something beyond human comprehension, I'd be happy to help, but, oh well! Don't feel bad. Do what you can, Princess Maria."

"I will."

A solemn silence settled over the room.

Alka broke it by changing the conversation. "Settin' that aside..." She pointedly wrung out her robe. Her tone made it very clear this was her primary concern.

"Now riddle me this, Marie. Ya knew perfectly well that crystal was a teleportation gate, so why was it at the bottom of a well? Whaddaya have to say for yourself?!"

"Oh." Marie finally remembered her impulsive fit of rage.

"I mean, I'll be tarred and feathered, even in my old age! ...Here I am, coming a-running to praise ya for sticking to your guns—and imagine my surprise when I found myself in a well."

"I—I may have gotten carried away. I regret it now."

Alka smiled broadly. "Why are you so frightened? I'm not angry, Marie."

"M-Master..." Alka's generosity had Marie on the brink of tears.

"…Well, and I've already cast 'nother curse on ya. You'll end one in ten sentences with *meow*. I ain't angry any longer."

"What?! Right before the day I settle everything *meow*?!" When Marie heard this last word, she turned bright red and burst into tears for real. "Aughhhhh! How could you do that to *meeeeoow*?!"

"Well, ain't that somethin'. Twice in a row! You're lucky."

"Am not! My luck ended the day I met you!"

"Well, consider it punishment for makin' Lloyd sad. Enjoy."

Marie cringed. Alka grinned.

"Oh, right. I near about forgot. Leave Lloyd to me on the day of the festival. I'll take care of him. Hunky-dory. You relax and focus on settling things. If ya die, I'll collect your bones and put them out with the hazardous trash."

And then Alka vanished into her crystal before Marie could point out that she clearly just wanted to run around the festival with Lloyd.

"You demon *loli* grandmaaaaa!"

As the first of the stars began to appear on the night sky, the witch's howl echoed across the town.

Chapter 5

An Egregious Mistake: Suppose You Mistook Someone Else for Your Date Because They Looked Nothing like Their Profile Picture

The foundation-day festival in the Kingdom of Azami was the main event of the spring season. With festivities on the days before and after the fair, it was three sleepless nights of celebratory fun.

"Lloyd, wanna hit this festival? I'll buy you a candy apple!"

The noise of the festival drifted through the shop windows. Lloyd was looking depressed as he cleaned up shop.

"Oh, Chief…no, I think I'm good. I'd better watch over the store."

"But ya always have a hankering for candy apples! Would you rather have a candy banana? Come on, up on yer feet. Let's go!"

"Er, no, the type of candied fruit isn't the issue."

"I see… Then I reckon you want a chocolate-covered banana! When ya see me taking a long, sensual bite of that vaguely indecent shape, you'll…and then I'll see you do the same…it's a win-win situation!"

"Erm, I'm not quite sure what you're talking about, but I'm pretty sure it isn't… Anyway, I'm just…not in the mood today. Sorry."

With that, Lloyd moved to the kitchen and started washing dishes, wiping them so clean that they definitely didn't need to be wiped any more. The sparkling kitchen was reaching model-home levels.

His heart isn't in it, eh? …But I figure if he's doing nothing, he can't stay calm—so he's washin' up instead. I suppose anyone with a moral compass like him would find it unbearable piddle-paddling while the fate of the country remains at large.

Alka stared at his back, thinking hard—most likely about how to cheer him up.

Eek! Oh, darn. He's so cute when he's gloomy! Oh, lordy! It's stoking my maternal instincts! It's stoking them so hard, smoke's about to come sputterin' out!

Of course, she wasn't sputtering smoke or whatever. With her maternal instincts (LOL) on fire, Alka sneaked up behind Lloyd, snatched him up with her beyond-human power, and hauled him outside.

The streets were always bustling, but during festival time, foreign tourists flooded to town, giving the streets an entirely different feel. The sweet scent of caramelized sugar mingled and mixed with the odors of frying meat. Alka hopped up and down with excitement after she'd finally put Lloyd down.

"Oh! This place is poppin'!" Alka raised her voice to compete with the noise around them, and her smile was every bit as big.

"...Yeah." Lloyd was the diametric opposite.

Alka looked at him, the wheels in her mind turning quickly.

Welp, I reckon the best cure for Lloyd's depression is the festival! And! He'll see firsthand that I'm amazin'! I'll earn his love and respect! And then tonight! With the sweet feelin' of liberation at the festival! The two of us! Alone in a secluded room! Something's bound to happen!

(It seems like the real festival was happening inside Alka's mind. Where'd that secluded room come from anyway?)

Ahhh... The prime setup! I reckon I've never seen one better! Yessiree, even though I've been around a hundred years...

Alka suddenly grew depressed by her lifetime of failures, and Lloyd didn't let that mood shift go unnoticed.

"Uh, Chief? You okay? Are the crowds getting to you?"

"N-no, I'm fine! ...Wait, I ain't fine. Oh geez. Gettin' tousled around in a crowd is so exhausting! We should definitely try out that shooting game! For nourishment and physical recovery! Come on, Lloyd!"

"Huh? Does target practice help? Wait, Chief! Don't yank on my arm so hard! You seem fine!"

Alka dragged him forcefully to the stall, where she threw down some coins, calling to the owner in a voice far younger than her usual one. "Hey, mister! I'm fixin' to try this game! I'm only nine, ya hear! Do I get a discount?!"

"Yep, you sure do! It's just one coin for you! Here's your gun—just don't point it at anyone, all right?"

Once she'd successfully obscured her real age by a full century, Alka gave him a phony grin and took the gun, making a big show of handling it clumsily, and fired in a random direction.

"Aww! I reckon I'm too short to see! Can I make my friend here pick me up?"

This latter half was delivered with a naughty smirk, but luckily, the owner missed it. He replied peppily, "Sure thing!"

...Permission granted.

"All righty, Lloyd!"

"Yes?"

"Pick me up!"

"Uh...?"

Alka had both arms flung up and ready for him, a twisted grin on her lips. Lloyd hesitated, but it was his chief's orders...or a total abuse of her authority, at the very least. After a brief internal struggle, Lloyd awkwardly put his hands on her waist, lifting her up high.

"Uh, excuse me...like this?"

"Yeehaw! ...No, Lloyd, you ain't gotta hold back! I reckon status doesn't matter in a festival! Squeeze me as tight as you want!"

"T-tight...uh, well...then..." He put his hands around her childish waist, squeezing her enough to crease her robe. He looked very embarrassed, afraid to look up, and kept his eyes cast down.

"Oh myyyyyy! Whoo-hoo!" This display of passion caused Alka to thrash her pigtails around. "No, more! I reckon you can go tighter than that, Lloyd!"

She had a taste for it now and wanted more.

"More? ...I dunno."

"Don't give up just yet! You gotta thwart social standing! It's a must! If one gives up on that, I reckon the festival might as well end!"

This argument made no sense at all to him, but Lloyd fumbled his way to a tighter grip.

After she'd been thoroughly manhandled, the *loli* grandma let out a heated gasp. She finally came to rest, held sideways like a princess—a pose that was definitely and utterly unrelated to target practice.

"Mwa-ha-haaahhh...heh-heh...heh-heh-heh...I suppose I'll settle for that."

...The sloppy look on Alka's face was hardly "settling" for anything.

But once she raised the gun again, a steely glint appeared in her eyes as she took aim at the most expensive-looking doll on the top shelf.

"Oh, that knight in armor looks cool!" Lloyd exclaimed, visibly excited. "You can see how detailed it is, even from here! Wow, workmanship in the city is amazing!"

"Figured," Alka muttered.

That's exactly the sort of thing he likes. I'm sure it's rigged to prevent it from toppling over, but I gotta earn his love and respect! And next up—his hand in marriage! It's all for a good cause!

Her brain was so lovestruck that she'd somehow gone from target practice straight to the altar. Alka scratched a quick series of runes, boosting the gun's power.

Force, speed, friction, spread...I reckon that's enough power. I call it the Love Burst!

Alka opened her eyes wide and pulled the trigger without a moment of hesitation.

An instant later...

Blam! A noise that should never come from a cork gun erupted through the stall.

Thwack! The bullet hit the target doll.

Pwww! And ricocheted off the figurine.

Crasshhhhhhhh! Then, the entire shelf of prizes collapsed to the ground.

"…Er, what?" The owner gaped.

Lloyd and Alka both went stiff.

There was a long silence. Then Alka rolled onto the floor, snatched the knight—which she'd decapitated entirely—and held it out to Lloyd, heedless of the stares from the crowd.

"A Dullahan doll!"

"Is not! You clearly blew the head off!"

"A secret character trait! It was a Dullahan all along! A curse from the land of dead!"

"This is the first I've heard of it!"

"L-let me try again! This time, I won't break any…"

"But, Chief." Lloyd pointed at the pile of broken prizes and the owner—all damaged beyond repair. The only part of the booth left intact was the gun in Alka's hands.

"…Um, mister?"

"…May I just go cry in a corner somewhere?"

He slunk off, drifting toward a shadowy corner like a ghost. He'd likely expected those prizes to last the full three days. If you can imagine a store manager forgetting to order stock on the headline item of a flyer, you could guess how he felt in that moment.

"Well, movin' right along! Next up!"

Meanwhile, Alka had the excessive optimism of a baseball coach in the middle of a losing streak. In her hundred-plus years alive, she'd gotten the art of forgetting all inconveniences down pat.

But her optimism would lead only to tragedy.

For the *loli* grandma's abuse of ancient runes would annihilate one stall after another.

From a balcony in the castle, the king was gazing down at the hustle and bustle of the first night of the festival. Two men stood behind him.

One was a silver-haired soldier with a resolute face and a scar running down his cheek: Merthophan Dextro. The other was a large man with a chiseled body: the former royal guard, Chrome Molybdenum.

Chrome approached the king from behind, kneeling and bowing his head.

"It has been some time, Your Majesty. My name is Chrome Molyb-denum, and I once served as the head of the royal guards. I'm here to ask that you allow me to return to active duty."

"..........." The king said nothing.

"I've heard war with the Jiou is approaching, and you need all the forces you can muster. I may not have much to offer, but if I am able to help, I have resolved to do so."

".............." Again, the king said nothing.

"That's enough, Chrome," Merthophan interjected. "I believe His Majesty has heard your plea. But I'm sure your abrupt request for an audience at this hour has angered him."

"...Is that the truth?"

"Yes. Await further word, Chrome. I'm sure you will soon be back in—"

"Is that really the truth, Merthophan?!" Chrome boomed.

Merthophan flinched, clearly rattled by this sudden burst of anger as Chrome's voice echoed across the balcony, fading into the noise of the crowds below them.

"What's got into you, Chrome? It's not like you to be so rude when you stand before—"

Before he could even finish, Chrome's iron fist swung toward him. Merthophan never stood a chance, and he was flung directly into the king, who didn't budge in the slightest.

"What the hell do you think you're doing, Chrome?!"

"*I'm* being rude?! Look at yourself, Merthophan! Since when do you not take a knee before His Majesty? Let me ask you again, Merthophan! Is that really the truth?" he choked out, as if his heart was breaking. A look of sadness crossed Chrome's face. "Have you really turned the king into a puppet to start a war?"

Realization dawned on him. Merthophan slowly staggered to his feet, swiping away the blood from the corner of his mouth as his expression grew stony once more.

"...Yes."

A low growl rumbled across the night, reverberating through the balcony. "............"

"You hardly need to ask me why, Chrome. Those fools have let the Jiou Empire do whatever they please, refusing to retaliate, much less go to war. I felt making him a puppet would be for the benefit of the realm."

"Merthophan..."

"Join me, Chrome. Even if you spread news of this, it'll only be taken up by the local gossip magazine. You're the proprietor of a cafeteria now. Don't forget that."

"............"

"This is the only way the realm can truly achieve peace. Please, Chrome."

Merthophan's soft pleas faded to silence.

Then...a high voice broke through the tension, seemingly out of place.

"Oh my! Did ya hear that? I wonder how much that bit of info is worth, m'lady. At least a hundred thousand!"

"With that much, Sir Lloyd and I could have three glorious weddings, at the very least!"

Riho and Selen stumbled in from the next room, chattering like it was a girl's night out.

"Riho Flavin...and Selen Hemein. And...who are you...?"

The last person to step onto the balcony was cloaked in black robes—Marie the Witch. She removed her fake glasses as she answered his question.

"Nice to meet you, Mr. Mastermind. I'm Maria Azami. These days, I call myself the Witch of the East Side, Marie."

"The princess, you say...?"

Merthophan's hand slipped down to his sword on instinct. Riho and Selen silently stepped between the princess and the colonel.

"We've got more than just the word of a former royal guard in a ridiculous apron. We've got the word of a missing princess... They'll believe that."

Riho raised her mechanical arm. "They may call me a villain, but you've crossed a line that I never would, Colonel."

Merthophan chuckled—as if he didn't have a care in the world about how many people appeared.

He didn't care if he died here.

There was no stopping the war.

His eyes told them everything as he raised his sword.

"I figured you were the one interfering with my plans, Your Highness... But you're too late to stop the war."

"Come again?"

"Don't play me for a fool. I used explosives to seal the road and blamed the Jiou Empire for it. I have no idea how you managed to clear up that mess, but that caused people to lose their desire for war. It was a major setback for my little scheme."

"Uh," Marie huffed, trying to remember, before she responded as if this whole thing was no biggie.

"That was Lloyd."

"What?"

"He went shopping to the west and found a crowd milling around the road, so he cleared it in, like, an hour."

"......" Merthophan's eyebrows twitched, but he recovered not long after. "Be that as it may! I don't know how, but you also ruined my plans to blame the dammed-up river on the Jiou Empire! That one impressed me. I'll give you that."

"That was also Lloyd."

"What?"

* * *

"Like, he found some merchant whose ship had run dry 'cause the water level had dropped, so he said he made it rain for them."

". . . . ."

"Basically, all I actually did was gather information… Bit by bit."

". . . . ."

"Oh, and I hate to say it, but apparently you panicked when you thought I was getting in your way and hired some local delinquents to find the princess…and that's how we figured out you were behind this."

". . . . ."

"And because Lloyd just so happened to beat up those same guys when they came after him, they coughed out everything voluntarily when they caught sight of him."

At this, Merthophan's shoulders began to tremble—in laughter. A self-deprecating smile crossed his lips. A rare display of emotion squeezed past his facial muscles.

"Heh-heh-heh…I see. So Lloyd Belladonna is an assassin you sent after me? …You had me totally fooled… It never made sense for someone as strong as him—"

Before he could praise her any further, Marie apologetically interrupted him. "I hate to say this…"

"…I think I'd rather not hear it, thank you very much."

"He actually has nothing to do with this. He wants to be a soldier because of his favorite novels."

Merthophan fell to his knees like a pitcher who'd given the other team a home run when all the bases were loaded. Everything that had happened had been a fluke: His own bad luck had done him in. All his resolve and confidence were gone…

"Merthophan! Cease your resistance! We have the means to free the king! And we're starting to feel sorry for you for…a lot of reasons! Surrender!"

But as Chrome offered this sympathetic appeal, a sinister laugh erupted out of the king himself.

"**Heh. Heh. Heh.**"

"*Ngh!*"

His chuckle spawned from the bowels of the earth—from darkness—and made all who heard it anxious with fear. All present felt their hair rising and braced themselves for the worst.

The king slowly turned, belly wobbling, and stared at Marie with eyes like night.

"**—I thought I sensed magic power... I see! The princess has come trotting back to the castle to make herself useful.**"

His aura seemed hardly human. They all took a step back.

"Merthophan! What did you do to him?!" Chrome boomed.

"I just tried to make him my puppet—"

Before he could finish, a bolt of energy surged out of the king's hand, blowing Merthophan away and slamming him into the wall so hard that it cracked. As he crumpled to the ground, he coughed and groaned in pain.

"**I tricked him into undoing my seal. Upon my revival, I took possession of a very powerful man to avoid being sealed again. And all the while, this fool never realized he was the real puppet.**"

"Uh...what are—?"

"**In truth, I was the one who attacked your village and people to stir up a grudge against the king. I didn't care who served me—anyone with enough spite for him would have done the job.**"

"No! You can't mean...! Back then? When the merchant said he had just the thing that would help me get revenge? It was you!"

"**Did that not strike you as suspicious? An item that could control a king? Did you really think something that could allow a human to control monsters would be for sale on the sidewalk?!**"

"Well, now that you mention it...gah..."

With an agility unfathomable for his rotund body, the king lunged at Merthophan in a single bound, grasping his entire head in one hand.

As Merthophan's face twisted in pain, the expression on the king's face showed no trace of humanity.

"But you've served your purpose. With so many people gathered at this festival—their souls will be wreathed in despair and become the offerings I need to fully regain my powers."

With an expression of despair and grief, Merthophan looked like he'd lost his grasp on sanity. He stared at the king with hollow eyes.

"And don't you worry. I'll make sure your little war will happen—as a one-sided slaughter. Oh, my horde of monsters will annihilate everyone, no matter their allegiance to a country! Serve me as best you can, Meth-what's-your-face."

With that, a green pattern emerged all over Merthophan's body: It seemed when a human's mind gave out, he could turn them into a monster.

"I...was wrong. I just wanted the realm to..."

An insectile exoskeleton began to appear around Merthophan as the king released him, dropping him to the ground, and turned to walk away. He sneered over his shoulder.

"Until my minions finish consuming your souls, I advise you follow the footsteps of your king—lie back and do nothing..."

As she heard his ominous warning, Selen noticed the bustle of the festival below them had turned into bloodcurdling screams. When she peered outside, she witnessed countless insects swarming the town.

"This is bad! There are insectile monsters everywhere!"

"Your Highness, please go after His Majesty! If you can free him, this will all die down!" Chrome shouted just as Merthophan, covered in that monstrous visage, threw himself at them with uncanny speed.

"Not happening!"

Riho jabbed her hand into Merthophan's torso, but he whipped her off of him like it was nothing.

"Eek!" She skidded across the floor.

"Riho?!"

"That…was nothing. Go on, Your Highness! We'll handle this!"

This was no time to fret and worry. Marie needed to save the king.

"And fast!" Riho urged.

Marie spun around and sprinted after him, down into the palace corridor that she'd walked through as a child. But this wasn't the right moment to savor her homecoming. She swerved through the door to pursue the possessed king into the audience chamber.

When she skidded to a stop, she was in a vast, solemn space without a single human present.

Only the monster. The king. Her father.

"…*Hmph*, **you dare follow me?**" With a green pattern stretched across his husky figure, the king settled into his gaudy throne.

"I want my father's body back."

That began the dual between the witch and the possessed king.

When he waggled his fingers, a crack ran down the ceiling, raining bits of plaster. Marie managed to dodge the falling debris and slapped him with a wind spell. But it affected him less than a refreshing breeze, and he returned the favor with a gale.

Her body lifted up from the ground and rammed into a wall.

They fought for nearly an hour: the king sitting on his throne as Marie continued her attacks, trying to find a chance to use a rune. But for all her efforts, she still hadn't been able to get him to stand.

Marie was starting to look tired.

"**…You're quite a woman. But don't worry. You'll be a useful tool for ruling other countries, and I will treat you well—as a human cannon. With your ability to use runes, we'll be able to gather souls effectively. You have only yourself to blame. When this man still had control, he was able to help you escape. You were a fool to return.**"

The king held up a hand, and the sinister green pattern writhed across it. Marie stood tall opposite him—absolutely furious.

"A tool?! You think any human would stand for that? Get out of my father! It's time you struck out on your own! Before I yank you out of there and turn you to ash!"

"You talk the talk—how...human. Nothing has changed since ancient times: Humans have always known how to bark—"

"Shuddup! Ancient times? Blah blah blah! Anyone who spews that kind of shit is incompetent! And that green ink crap on my father's face is pissing me off! I'm gonna get that off him right now!"

"I admire your spirit... But I am not like my minions."

That arrogance will prove your downfall. All right! I'm about to turn the tables!

Marie waved her fingers, causing symbols to appear out of thin air as she released an ice spell. In an instant, the stone walls of the audience chamber were covered in frost. A pillar of ice erupted from under his feet in the next second. But he knocked it aside with one arm.

As he watched the ice shards scatter, his lips twisted and his gelatinous belly shook with laughter.

"...Heh-heh-heh, I see you aren't afraid of injuring your father."

Her cold expression didn't betray the fact that Marie was grinning on the inside.

I knew that wouldn't harm you. Go on being smug, buddy.

Once again, her fingers waggled to unleash a different spell—this time calling forward flames.

Columns of fire raged throughout the room. But once again, he brushed it aside with a wave of his hand as though he were handling a few paltry sparks.

"When ice doesn't work, you try fire... How lazy... Mm?"

Just as the flames licked the shattered remains of the ice pillar and consumed them, the area was enveloped in a thick fog.

"...Trying to blind me?"

This was all part of Marie's plan. As she hid in the mist, she ran her fingers across the back of her hand—in a strategy deviating from the rest.

The *disenchant* rune was the one way to release the king from evil without harming him. She was powering up her strongest attack.

I've practiced this over and over...it takes maybe thirty seconds, tops. Then...

With a pale blue light wreathed around her hand, Marie dashed straight toward him as the mist grew thin. When the king saw the light on her hand, his face contorted again—but not in a smile this time.

"What is that?! What is that awful light!"

"I'll end this once and for all!"

Just one more step. Marie's fists were inches from landing.

In that moment, the king's expression changed from merciless to gentle as he tenderly whispered, "—Oh, how you've grown, Maria."

"————*Gh!*"

A momentary hiccup in her attack.

The king didn't let it go unnoticed, slamming into her hard and sending her flying all the way to the doorway.

"Gahh…!"

As she writhed in pain, his expression went blank again and his voice became unnatural once more.

"You're a fool… Such a fool. You were one step from getting me and accomplishing whatever you were planning."

With a bellowing guffaw, he yanked her arm, crushing her palm as blithely as he might ball up a sheet of paper before dunking it in a trash can. As she let out a silent shriek, Marie desperately ripped her hand free from his grasp and scrambled away, backing up like a frightened child. The king sneered down at her pathetic retreat.

"Augh…dammit…"

It was unlikely that she'd be able to write another rune. All she could do was stare at her crunched fingers with regret.

"Consider it a blessing to die at the hand of your father."

She was out of options. Marie looked up at the ceiling in despair.

A certain boy's innocent little face floated into her mind.

She bit her lip, snapping her fading consciousness back on track to brace herself to fight again. When Marie managed to squeeze out a spell from her broken fingers, another ice pillar blasted from below at the king's feet, but it was much smaller than the one before.

"How futile."

"I haven't had a chance to apologize to Lloyd! I can't let myself die here!"

"Yet, you stand and fight, instead of trying to flee."

"Don't be absurd! How could I call myself royalty if I turned my back on an enemy of the realm?"

"I respect that—and in return, I shall torture you until you beg me for your life. Until you turn your back and bolt away in tears."

"Ha! All paths of retreat are already lost."

"Heh-heh-heh. Don't worry. This kingdom—nay, the very world—lies in the palm of my hand. Yes…"

He held a hand up, rising to a fever pitch.

"In the hand of *the demon lord, Abaddon*!"

Silence filled the audience chamber.

"…………"

Marie blinked back at him.

This was not the reaction that the demon lord had expected.

He grew confused. **"You could look more impressed, you know. Boring."**

"…………Why?"

"Why what?"

"………Why didn't you say so sooner?!" Marie whined, shouting like a lawyer making an objection.

"Mm? It seems I may have touched a nerve… But I was hoping to revel in your anger and despair."

"No, geez! I'm definitely angry, you asshole! Why didn't you just say so?! You're a demon lord! A DEMON? LORD? If I'd known that a couple of days earlier, I'd never have had to put myself through all that misery! This would have been EASY-PEASY LEMON SQUEEZY!"

"You certainly seem angry, but...not for the right reasons... Whatever, it's fine—"

"It is not fine! You know how much work I put into this?!"

Ignoring her injuries, Marie braced for combat.

"*Hmph*. Those will be your last words."

Whoosh.

Marie had turned and booked it out of there—totally turning her back on him, her robe streaming behind her, going as fast as she could.

"Huh? Hey, wait! What happened to royalty never retreating?! What about your pride?! Your dignity?!"

"That was ages ago! Long forgotten! Everything's different now, you damn demon lord! You're gonna regret being one! Just you wait!"

"Hey! That's not the standard line of someone retreating! Get your ass back over here!"

The situation had completely reversed itself. Now Marie was running toward the balcony, pursued by the demon lord Abaddon.

Marie sprinted, gritting her teeth at the stabbing pain in her broken fingers.

"Gotta get to Lloyd or the *loli* grandma! No matter what!"

An hour before this great escape...

"Well, Lloyd?! Ain't I just unbelievable?!"

Alka was clutching a mountain of prizes, looking very pleased with herself. But Lloyd was wearing an increasingly gloomy expression.

"Sure, but...I'm more in disbelief about that." Lloyd was pointing at a row of sobbing stall owners left in her wake, feeling sorry for all of them.

"It doesn't make sense...why would the goldfish start floating on their own? And why would they *leap* into the bowl?!"

"When she touched the cutouts, they practically fell out of their molds...!"

"She pulled the ticket for the grand prize even though I didn't put it in the pile!"

Well, maybe not the last one.

"Pretend you can't see 'em." Alka didn't even so much as glance toward the waiting room—for losers.

The duo hunkered down on a nearby bench.

Alka dumped her pile of prizes on the ground, grinning. But Lloyd looked as cheerless as ever—no, almost twice as somber as he had an hour ago. The cause of his melancholy mood was obvious. Plus, Alka was the only one enjoying herself here.

Bweh-heh-heh, we've had a blast! I reckon today was the day we got... somewhere...

Alka was pulling a full-on act of being clueless—playing the part of a major throwback—a necessary characteristic for any true *loli* grandma.

"I think it's time we went home."

"Wait a sec, Lloyd! There's still the main event!"

"The main event?"

"That's right! You can't have a festival without...!"

"Without what?"

"You guessed it! Chocolate-covered bananas!"

"...Does that even qualify as an event? It's just food."

Pushing aside his concerns, Alka pulled something out of her pocket—some sort of brown paste. If this was chocolate, it only raised more questions.

"I've already got the chocolate ready! Ne'er fear!"

"Uh...Chief...where's the banana?"

"Bweh-heh-heh! You know where it is. Don't make me spell it out."

Just as she was about to try and make up for a century of getting nowhere, screams rang out over the bustle of the festival.

Lloyd turned toward the sounds. Both listened carefully.

"H-help! Monsters!" "The monsters are rampaging through town!" "I don't wanna die!"

"Huh? M-monsters?"

"I hear tell something's gone wrong…we'd better take a look lickety-split."

Alka and Lloyd dashed toward the voices, parting through a crowd running the other way.

Lloyd grabbed ahold of someone passing by. "Um, what's going on?"

"R-run for it! A wh-whole bunch of monsters suddenly came swarming out of nowhere! Aaaaargh, they're heeeeeere!"

The festivalgoers went pale as they shrieked, scrambling toward the nearest city gate. The man had cast a pointed look at something before he followed suit.

Shnk, shnk, shnk.

A whole lot of giant locusts were approaching, mandibles snapping. When Lloyd traced the man's gaze, Lloyd tromped right on over.

"Hokay!"

And he swatted the swarm of locusts with a wave of his hand. They smacked into the wall and turned to ash. Only then did Lloyd get worried.

"This is bad, Chief! There're monsters nearby! And they're attracting all these bugs!"

In truth, the "bugs" themselves were monsters…but Alka looked at the locust swarm and stroked her chin.

"These locusts…hmm?"

Something seemed to be jogging her memory. But heedless of what was going on in Alka's mind, Lloyd looked downright grave.

"Hey, Chief…sorry, there's somewhere I need to be."

"Mm? Oh, what's gotten into ya?"

"I can't tell you everything, but…Marie's in trouble. And Selen and Riho, too…"

Alka knew exactly what he was talking about, but she made a big show of pressing him further. "Hmm, I ain't sure what that means, but, Lloyd—whaddaya think you can do?"

Lloyd hesitated for a moment before he turned toward Alka with a resolute look in his eyes.

What in tarnation?! My heart!

With more certainty than he'd shown about leaving the village, Lloyd stood with his back straight, a confident set in his jaw, and words filled with conviction.

"I have no idea!" he claimed.

"Har?!"

He had the spirit of a student who'd raised their hand to answer the problem on the blackboard only to admit they had no clue. It completely took the wind out of Alka's sails.

"But one thing I've learned recently is that there are times when even a weakling like me—especially a weakling like me—has to take action."

"Hmm…"

"I may be weak, and Marie may have saved me any number of times. Including when I almost got in a fight. But at the same time, she's taught me the importance of moving forward, even if you aren't sure how or where. That's why—" His cheeks flushed red as he finished in a heartfelt shout. "I dunno what I can do to help! But I do know that doing nothing is wrong! Even if Marie yells at me! Even if you try to stop me! Even if I'm weak—I have to go!"

With that, he spun around, bolting at top speed toward the castle. He'd launched off into a sprint with so much force, the pavement below him cracked in a trail behind him.

As Alka watched Lloyd go, she sighed.

"You never listen, do ya…but I reckon I've never seen you this worked up. You're growing up. I'd give you full marks if you weren't doing this for that idiot Marie."

Alka looked ready to shed a tear, but the crowd flowing toward her was only getting denser. The center of the festival must be a living hell right about now.

"So we're up against a demon lord, hmm…? Well, I'll bet my bottom dollar that it's probably a really weak one that he can handle… Dunno if that means we're lucky—for this kingdom or for my dumb student… Welp, if there's a demon lord involved, I can't just stand around."

©Nao Watanuki

She shook her head, then pulled out a small crystal, grinning. Her ear-to-ear smile was reflected in the polished surface.

"Death to anything that interrupts me gettin' it on with Lloyd… Time for a good old-fashioned rampage."

The town was overflowing with a sudden swarm of locust monsters. They were everywhere, and people trying to escape were boxed in. It was hell in every corner. Fortunately, festival security had soldiers all over the place, and casualties were kept to a minimum.

Meanwhile, Lloyd raced through the commotion to the castle and Marie. In fact, he was zooming past so fast that nobody even noticed him. Plus, everyone was preoccupied with fending off the monsters.

As Lloyd witnessed the state of the town, he thought, *This town's in a panic…but where are the monsters? Man, this sure is attracting a lot of bugs…*

He hustled through the crowd in fear of the unseen beasts as he swatted away bugs (monsters) in his path. And when he reached a narrow alley leading to the castle…

"Eeeck!" A short, shrill scream called out from the back.

Lloyd turned toward the noise.

"…H-huh? Oh, it's you. The part-timer," said Allan—an earlier competitor from an unfinished battle. He was crouched down, tense with fear.

"Er, Allan, was it?" Lloyd asked, looking confused. "What are you doing here?"

"Ha…ha-ha. This is sort of pathetic, I know."

"Were you hiding?"

"Not…exactly…no. Okay, look, fine. I was hiding. It's, uh, scary."

Lloyd couldn't hide his surprise. "*You're* scared? But you tried to fight me, and Selen…"

"Humans are one thing! …But, uh, monsters? A totally different story… Well, more like animals and bugs… Ever since I was a kid, I've always trained against people, you know, entering all those tournaments and stuff. But when I'm up against something on all fours, like a monster slithering along the ground...I don't even know how to begin to fight them."

"So when you said you had a goal..."

Allan nodded listlessly. "If I get promoted, I won't have to fight monsters. I can just train soldiers! I'll never stain the family name."

"But...everyone else is busy fighting these beasts right now."

"I know! I know what you're trying to say...and I want to help! But my body's all frozen!"

Lloyd realized Allan hadn't moved a muscle this entire time. His legs had given out—a familiar feeling that Lloyd knew all too well.

I felt the same way the first time I fought a monster...

Of course, these so-called monsters were threatening demon lords who'd descended into the mortal realm, and Lloyd knew just how hard it could be. He rebuked Allan, almost as if trying to convince himself.

"I'm scared, too... But...I've always admired soldiers, people who would keep moving forward no matter what."

"...That's right... You're the one who failed the admissions test."

"Yeah, I'll take it again next year...and right now, I'm going to help in any way I can."

No sooner had he declared his intentions than a giant locust came flying right at his back.

"Behind you!" Allan jumped up, trying to yank Lloyd out of the way. But before his hands could reach him...

"Excuse you! This is an important conversation. Shoo!"

With a satisfying *thwack*, the monster went flying.

"Look ou— Huh?" Allan gaped.

Lloyd turned back to him, continuing to speak earnestly. "You're right. Monsters are certainly scary. You could die fighting them. But—"

"Hold on! Wait a sec! That was a monster right there! What are you talking about?!"

"There, see? That's no good! You can't let yourself get so scared that you think any old thing's a monster! That's just an insect!"

"What? An…insect?"

"Yep! Regular old bug."

Allan's brain shut down.

When he finally spoke again, it was a strangled squeak. "Uh… no way…"

Lloyd flashed Allan his patented smile. "More importantly…see? You can move, after all."

"I…oh, wait." Allan seemed surprised to find himself on his feet.

"You're a soldier! You're stronger than I am. Maybe you're scared, and maybe I'm not in a position to say this, but…you have to try!"

And then Lloyd was gone with the wind.

When Lloyd was out of sight, Allan staggered out of the alley.

What's with *that kid? He said these monsters were just bugs? That's insane!*

He surveyed the scene, looking around to find the town in a state of panic. Because tourists from all over flooded to town for the festival, they didn't know their way around, which meant they had no idea where to go as they sprinted through the city willy-nilly, trying to get away.

Here and there, he saw soldiers desperately trying to guide the crowds, tend to their injuries, or fight the monsters. Allan witnessed civilians supporting each other, and he couldn't stand still any longer.

Argh…I'm pathetic. I've got to guide them or help the wounded at the very least! He scolded himself.

"Aiieee!" Just then, a shrill cry echoed over the din.

"Keep running!" someone yelled.

Allan turned his gaze against the flow of the crowd.

"H-help!"

In front of him, a giant six-yard locust covered in scales like moss was menacing a woman who'd fallen down. She'd missed her chance to escape and couldn't stand up as she struggled under its exoskeleton.

Allan looked around him, hoping to find someone else capable of fending it off, but he was the only person with a weapon. He knew what this meant.

He knew what he had to do. "If I don't help, she'll die."

At the same time, his legs were shaking so hard that he couldn't move. Allan had no idea how to even begin fighting anything that crawled along the ground.

...Dammit! Stop shaking! Come on, quads!

His efforts to motivate his body got him nowhere. He peeked around his surroundings, confirming for the umpteenth time that there wasn't anyone else there. Then he saw a reflection of himself in the window of a nearby building, looking like a frightened little brat.

...Pathetic... How could I ever get promoted?

Allan had tunnel vision on career advancement, which had all been an effort to avoid fighting monsters and casting mud on his family name.

But no superiors would ever promote the likes of me! I don't even deserve to call myself a soldier!

He pictured Lloyd from a moment before. Pushing his fears aside and forcing his legs to move, he focused his thoughts on the task at hand. At last, he started to advance.

"—Rahhh!"

Allan lunged toward the monster, swinging his ax and landing a blow on the beastly bug. With that came a spurt of some bodily fluid—not blood—and the monster turned toward him.

"Argh...crap!!" Through his screams, Allan swung again and again, but the monster showed no signs of fear.

And he knew why—it was because Allan himself was so obviously scared, in a position ready to flee at a moment's notice.

But I'm doing it! I will make *myself into a man! I refuse to be afraid of monsters!*

He'd certainly succeeded in annoying the monster enough that it let out a shrill cry and fought back. As it reared up, its full six yards loomed over Allan, threatening him—on two hind legs.

"Aiiiieeee!"

Its sheer size was enough to make the crowd around them shriek in horror. All except one.

"Heh-heh-heh-heh-heh!" Allan started laughing.

And an instant later, a powerful blow to its side split the monster in two, dissolving it into ash.

A cheer erupted from the crowd, and the woman came over, thanking him for saving her. But Allan was in no state to absorb any praise. He was breathing heavily, basking in the glow of his first victory.

"Looks…like I can do it after all!"

And with that, he went darting off, searching for other monsters— facing forward, confidence in his stride.

"I'm not scared anymore! I won't let you insects get away with this!"

Allan Toin Lidocaine's battle had only just begun.

Meanwhile, in the castle, Chrome had engaged the possessed Merthophan in combat. The viridescent pattern covering Merthophan was slowly turning into an exoskeleton.

"Kill me! For the peace of the realm!"

It seemed only his head remained under his control, and he was begging for death in a guttural growl. This only served to weaken Chrome's blows.

"Merthophan…"

And yet, despite his pleas, the demonic body was strong, its movements swift, and his sword swung at Chrome with deadly force.

Clang! Clang! Their weapons clashed two, three times and ground against each other. But his friend's grief-stricken face weakened Chrome's arms, and he was pushed back.

"Gah!" As his square frame was flung aside, Chrome let out a grunt. Riho dashed in, catching Merthophan's blade on her mechanical arm before it could finish Chrome off.

"Crap… With the monster possessing him, he's way stronger than before!"

Her mithril hand was creaking. Just then, an insect shell snapped around Merthophan's arm—a thick one, the size of a man's torso.

Even though mithril was far stronger than steel, her arm crumpled instantly under his grip.

"Seriously?!" she yelped, managing by a hairbreadth to slip away as she dragged Chrome after her.

Merthophan's body slowly crouched down, looking like a predator about to pounce on its prey. The shell was slowly covering the rest of him, making him look less and less human.

"Ugh...we're in trouble..."

At this, Selen broke her silence for the first time.

"Oh, we could really use Sir Lloyd's help right now..."

"...Yeah, this is no time to yak on and on! M'lady, summon Lloyd here right now!"

"Eh-heh-heh...leave this to me."

But Selen showed no signs of bolting out of there to find him. Instead, she walked directly toward Merthophan.

"Uh, hey! What do you think you're doing?"

"Isn't it obvious? This is how you summon Sir Lloyd."

The green shell became part of Merthophan's face. He was now a strange crustacean in a military uniform.

"K...cree-cree-cree...hshh...cree-cree!" What had once been Merthophan let out a string of cryptic nonwords.

And Selen was facing off against him, claiming she was calling Lloyd as she took her battle stance and looked suspiciously ready to fight. Riho was at a complete loss.

"What are you *doing*?! We need Lloyd here right now!"

"I know! Hurry up and attack me, Colonel Merthophan!"

Riho could not imagine what Selen was thinking as she managed to squeak, "What are you saying?!"

"Isn't it obvious? The hero always arrives to save his heroine in the nick of time. Come on, Colonel Merthophan! Place me in mortal peril!"

"Are you out of your *mind*?!"

Even at a time like this, Selen was Selen—totally committed and devastatingly delusional.

"I think it'd be way better if my clothes were torn up. Just enough to tease but not show anything… Oh, don't worry, I've got this belt."

As if in response—well, considering the circumstances, it likely wasn't *actually* in response, Merthophan whipped his hardened shell of an arm at Selen.

There was a loud *whoosh*, delivering a blow powerful enough to rip through her clothes and splatter her guts all over the walls.

"Don't be stupid, Selen…uh, huh?"

But the attack never hit her.

Shpp! Clanggg!

The cursed belt stopped Merthophan mid-attack. Just like it had Allan's. It writhed as though it were alive, reaching out and knocking the attack back.

A gloomy smirk crossed her lips. If asked whether Selen or Merthophan was the villain in this scene, most people wouldn't hesitate to reply: "Both."

"Eh-heh-heh-heh! As I thought! This belt is the red string binding us together! Now go on! Rip my clothes a little!"

But this thought didn't last long.

Shpp! Claaannngg! Shpp! Claaaanngg! Shppp! Claaaangg!

Selen didn't appear to be in any sort of peril, ever. Not one attack made it past the belt, and her clothing remained stubbornly intact.

"Just you wait! Any minute now! I bet my outfit will start taking damage soon!"

But the belt didn't seem to heed her wishes, blocking every attack with precision.

"Uh, m'lady," Riho interjected. "Is that cursed belt stopping him without any input from you? That's…pretty amazing…"

Chrome frowned, looking like he'd just remembered something.

"Come to think of it…the legends of Kunlun said something about a treasure that could protect you from all ill will… Could it be that belt?"

With her plans actively ruined by this so-called treasure, gratitude was the last thing on Selen's mind.

"No way! How am I supposed to get to the scene where I hug Sir Lloyd when he comes to rescue me?!"

"How should I know?! Just…keep Merthophan's attacks focused on you! I'll go try and find Lloyd!" Riho started to drag her injured body on the ground.

"Hey! That's not the plan! I wanted to call him!"

"Yo! Don't follow me! If I get in the middle of your fight, I'm done for!"

In the middle of this, a new figure literally leaped onto the balcony.

"Uh, sorry to show up so late… Oh, Riho!"

It was the boy in question—Lloyd.

"L-Lloyd?!"

He'd cleared dozens of yards from the stairs to the balcony in a single bound, as if he'd heard them calling. Riho couldn't hide her surprise.

"Sorry! I figured it was an emergency, so I just jumped on in! …Oh god! Riho, you're hurt! Hold on!" Lloyd dashed over to her side and began tending to her injuries.

When she found herself suddenly in his arms, Riho turned bright red.

"Oh, no, uh… These'll heal with a little spit! I'm fine!"

Lloyd looked a little rattled and turned pink himself, but then he made up his mind and moved his face closer to her wound.

"Uh…spit? O-okay, if you say so… Like this?"

He appeared just about ready to kiss her wound when Riho hastily stopped him.

"No, no! I mean, I'll do it myself!"

The situation was threatening to turn X-rated, as they played out a scene that Selen imagined for herself.

"You've got the wrong giiiiiirl!" she shrieked as her belt slapped away another round of Merthophan's attacks. It goes without saying that she desperately wanted to trade places with Riho.

Lloyd's head snapped up when he heard her scream, but once again, he failed to answer her desires.

"Oh, Selen! You look fine. Good job!"

"Sir Lloyd! Right now! I have a terrible pain! In my heaaaaart!"

But her cries were drowned out by the little slappy noises of the belt.

After he'd confirmed that Selen was in safe hands, Lloyd next found Chrome crumpled against the wall.

"Wait, why is the boss here?! Are you okay?!"

"Lloyd…? Why…are *you* here?"

"I came to help…but I'm not sure what I can do."

"I see… As you can see, I slipped up. We can use the help."

"That path is a road of infinite hardship—with no chance of any offspring, Sir Lloyd!"

"Don't make things more complicated, Belt Princess!"

"Oh, you don't get to talk, Riho! Not after savoring that moment with him!"

"…Sorry." *Blush.*

"…Er, what?"

"…I'm really sorry, Selen." *Blush.*

"Don't turn red! Why aren't you denying it?! Now I *really* feel like I've lost!"

Ignoring the two as they gossiped (?), Chrome thrust his chin at Merthophan.

Lloyd looked at the green shell and military uniform with a nod. "—I think I get the general idea." He took a step closer to Merthophan, looking grim.

"………Ll………oyd…" He grunted.

Lloyd had on a painful expression. "I think I get the gist of things… But you're a soldier… You're supposed to protect the people. What are you doing?"

He was moving nearer to the possessed colonel, inching closer, one step at a time—calling on the ideals that made Merthophan want to be a soldier in the first place.

"I'm sure…you once wanted to protect people's lives and smiling faces… That's why you became a soldier, right? Not for this."

Merthophan's expression was slowly melting back into its human form again as memories of when he first enlisted surfaced in his mind.

That's right…I…

And the shell covering him peeled away, crumbling.

"Merthophan…," Chrome called out to his old friend.

For the sake of Azami…for my village, for the smiles of the citizens…

"Colonel Merthophan," Selen encouraged, relieved to see her officer once more.

"No…war…a world of plenty…"

"Merthophan the gentle sir," Riho choked out.

A large hunk of shell fell to the floor. Behind it, his face reflected a new kind of sadness on it.

"I…"

As cracks ran across the rest of the exoskeleton, Merthophan regained his senses, freeing himself from the confines of the shell.

"And plus…," Lloyd added, once Merthophan's attacks came to a halt. "What kind of soldier gets so drunk that they put on a silly cosplay and go on a rampage?! You're failing at a basic human level!"

""""Where'd that come from?!"""""

"Seriously! At a time like this? Helloooo? There are monsters in town! Not that I've seen any. But you're just ignoring that threat? And wearing this cosplay? And drinking so much that your face literally turns green? Boss, you've got to cut him off sooner! I know it's a festival and all, and I get that you're trying to run a business, but you've got to think of your customers! What did you even drink? Oh, was it that green apple cider?"

*   *   *

"Cree-cree-cree-cree-cree!"

Merthophan was instantly enveloped in a new shell, which seemed even larger than the last one.

"We were one step away! Why'd you ruin it, Lloyd?! The mood was right and everything! You'd almost made his heart human again!"

"Lloyd! Start over, from the top! For Merthophan's sake!"

"Huh? From the getting drunk and wearing a cosplay part?"

"Are you doing this *on purpose*?!"

"Cree-cree-cree! I didn't drink anything!" wailed the regressed ex-Merthophan.

"Look, just because I hit the nail on the head doesn't mean you get to throw a tantrum!" Lloyd scolded, slapping him silly. The creature's head twisted in a very unnatural direction.

"Cree!"

"I may be weak, but I'm not about to lose to a drunken cosplayer!"

As he continued to mutter, "Geez, did you get drunk at the festival, too, Boss?" Lloyd pulled a handkerchief out of his pocket—the one with the runes on it.

"Let's get this filth off you, at the bare minimum. Stand still!"

Lloyd grabbed Merthophan's arm with enough force to crack it and began vigorously rubbing his face with the cloth.

"Cree-cree…aaah…"

Merthophan let out an odd sigh as the *disenchant* rune peeled his shell off, causing the pieces to fall away, turn into light, and vanish.

It was almost beautiful, but at the center of it all, Merthophan was left lying unconscious. He was looking like he really had to pee, like he had something else to say. Presumably being treated like a drunken cosplaying patriot had been one indignity too many.

"Wore himself out rampaging and fell right asleep, huh? Someone needs to learn some moderation. Uh…where's Marie?"

Chrome rubbed his exasperated expression off his face. "Oh, right!"

©Nao Watanuki

he exclaimed, as if he'd just remembered something. "Yes! She's in back, fighting the monster that's possessing the king!"

"Wh-what?! Alone? And you're all standing around playing with a drunk?!"

"Oh, uh…sorry."

Lloyd dismissed Merthophan's monster form as an alcoholic mess— causing those around him to be astounded once again by how overpowered he was.

But the stunned silence was interrupted by a shriek as someone came busting into the room.

"Run for iiiiiit! Whoa! Arghh…!"

It was Marie, booking it from the grasp of the demon lord. Without a hint of royal or feminine dignity, she tripped over Merthophan and skidded across the floor.

"Whoa! Wh-what happened, Marie?!" Riho asked, confused by Marie's sudden appearance. It's a bit like when your friend unexpectedly logs into the chat.

"Change of plans! Plan B! Drop a smoke signal!"

"Calm down! We don't have a plan B! And smoke goes up, not down!"

"Strategic retreat! We've gotta get to Lloyd or the *loli* grandma pronto—!"

"M-me?" Lloyd squeaked, surprised to hear his name.

"L-Lloyd?! Why are you here?!" Marie's eyes nearly popped out of her head.

He had on an apologetic look. "Sorry!" he said, wincing, as he continued to plead with her. "I know you said not to come, but I couldn't just do nothing! 'Cause, like, I thought if I continued to twiddle my thumbs, I'd never be able to grow up!"

Then he tensed up, waiting for a scolding.

"Welcome!" Marie shouted, throwing her arms out and doing a few quick dance steps like a character in costume at an amusement park.

"Er…" Lloyd gaped at her. What happened to their fight the day before?

But from behind Marie's fantastical display, the demon lord Abaddon strode in, belly jiggling with every step.

"Hmph...you took that man down? No matter. I'll just kill you all myself!"

His aura was overwhelming Marie, Chrome, Selen, and Riho, who all cowered before him. His inhuman nature was so ominous that it was stifling, and their eyes trailed after him silently. Well, all except Lloyd.

"Oh, um, excuse me. We're in a dangerous situation, so you should really hide somewhere." After urging the demon lord to evacuate, he turned back to the others. "...Now, Marie, where's this monster? I may not be much help, but I can at least be a decoy or...!"

The king gawked at him. There was a long silence, and then he decided to just start over.

"Hmph...you took that man down? No—"

"Um, sorry! There's a monster nearby! You really should hide! He's apparently possessed the king!"

"—That's me!" he bellowed in his stilted way.

Lloyd gave him a look of skepticism that clearly said, *What the* heck *are you talking about?*

"Sir...come on. Even I know that's not true. I mean, I walk past the statue of the king every day on my way to work... He's much taller, and he doesn't have a gut like you. He's pretty fit. You should really take a look someday."

The statue in the town square was loosely modeled after the king—Marie called it a tribute to his vanity. Lloyd had never seen the real man, so who could blame him for this small mistake? Well, he was now, but...

As for the monster possessing this sad sack of gluttonous flesh, he was left in disbelief. **"Uhh..."** He groaned laboriously.

Paying his confusion no heed, Lloyd kept going. "...Oh, I see! There's a weird look in your eyes... Are you also drunk? Gotcha. That's why you're wearing that king cosplay...for the festival... Oh wow, give me a break with this whole demon lord joke."

"**...Cosplay?**" The demon lord seemed confused by the unfamiliar term.

"Oh, now that I look at you, your complexion isn't so good. You spilled some green apple cider, didn't you? Is everyone sloshed around here? Hurry up and take refuge somewhere." Lloyd gave a few helpful pointers to the root of all evil before turning back to Marie.

"B-by the way," he stammered, looking nervous. "Is this monster possessing the king still a problem?"

He was nervous and afraid of the beast, which still hadn't made its grand appearance (LOL). Marie gave him a long look, then an idea must have hit her, as she smiled, boasting, "Y-yeah, it was a real tough one!"

"Oh, then you already...?"

"That I did! It was all *blam* and *pow*, and I hit back with a little bit of the you-know-what and blanched it for a few secs. But in the end, it was no match for me! I'm pretty good at this, you see! I'll have to crack open that bottle of mead from my birth year tonight!"

"Blanched...?"

"Yep, and just as I finished this death match, when I was barely able to get to my feet, this oafish cosplayer shows up to ruin the moment—reeking of booze, to boot! I didn't know what to do!"

"I *knew* he was drunk! You can tell from his voice."

"Exactly! And he just wouldn't leave me alone! It was awful. He stinks, and his hygiene is *blegh*...Lloyd, could you wipe him down with that thing for me?"

"Oh, that thing? Sure, got it."

The demon lord started protesting. "**Hey! Princess! I'm not drunk! Why did you say—?**"

But Lloyd gently shushed him. "Princess? Marie's a witch, sir. Princesses don't live off canned food or get down on their hands and knees with a silly face. You really are drunk!"

"Ha-ha-ha...goddammit..." Marie cursed in tears over this brutal takedown of her very existence.

Meanwhile, Lloyd whipped out his handkerchief, quickly sketching a *disenchant* rune, and attempted to wipe the demon lord's face.

"Stop! What are you doing! Stay back!"

The monster swung his arm in a hasty attack, but Lloyd easily deflected it.

"Yes, yes, you're drunk... Settle down."

When the monster watched as his arm sailed through the air to puncture a hole in the concrete, his expression changed from hollow-eyed to horrified.

"Augh...stay away from me...!"

But this didn't dissuade Lloyd, who calmly started wiping the green stuff from Abaddon's face, scrubbing it right off. Chunks started falling to the floor and turning to ash.

"You little—how dare you?! I-I'm vanishing? ...What have you done?!"

Lloyd looked slightly confused. "This? It's just a little cleaning hack."

"There's no waaaaay!"

As bits of the demon lord started to turn to ash and Abaddon's panic grew, Marie stepped in to deliver the final blow.

"Be gone, demon lord! At the hands of the humans you looked down on!"

"You little—!"

Marie's index finger cut through the air. "I'll tell you why you lost. You messed with my family...and you failed to take humanity seriously *meow*!"

"Why was there a cat noise?! You're the one not taking this serious—unhh," he groaned.

With the one-in-ten curse activating at the worst possible time, Abaddon dissolved into dust, leaving the body of the king behind.

".........Er......*meow*? Marie, are you drunk, too?"

"Uh, er...heh-heh-heh...........maybe a little?" To cover up her pathetic lie, Marie gave him a big hug.

"Er, hey? Marie?"

She put her lips to his bright red ears and whispered, "Thanks for coming to save me."

"All right, I think we all deserve an explanation—right after you get off of him!" Riho snapped.

"Didn't you spend ages convincing him *not* to get involved…?" Selen demanded.

Marie shuddered. *One demon lord down, and two to go…*

A few days after the monster incident, Allan Toin Lidocaine was summoned to a very imposing room in the palace, unable to disguise his trepidation.

"Sorry for making you wait, Allan."

When he turned toward the voice, Allan found a high-ranking officer in a perfectly starched uniform taking a seat at the desk before him.

Someone this high up called me in? ... What's going on?

With his mind reeling, Allan snapped to attention, and the officer began to explain.

"Allan Toin Lidocaine, was it? I'm told you proved yourself versatile and dynamic in this latest attack. You've saved many lives."

"Wha...? Th-thank you, sir!" he squeaked, taken aback by this sudden barrage of high praise.

"Your performance was of immeasurable value to our army. I can see why your family has been so decorated... You've certainly exceeded our expectations for their eldest son."

Allan was starting to think this was somewhat undeserved. But the officer's next words cleared that up.

"You see...there's some vexing chatter around town—people saying they were rescued by 'some random girl in town for the festival.' ...Stories about her slapping monsters around bare-handed or making meteors drop on them...nonsense, of course. I imagine it's been spread by scum attempting to undermine the army's reputation, ha-ha-ha!"

Oh, I get it... They have to save face. They can't just admit an outsider saved the day, so they want to make me into their hero.

Their plan was to prop him up and attempt to override the rumors circulating among the peasants. Allan wasn't sure about this. After all, he'd seen the truth with his own two eyes and knew how much worse things would have been without them.

"That's why we'd like to offer you some sort of reward. We've heard tell you're interested in rising through the ranks...and I imagine that it would be the talk of the town if someone from the decorated Lidocaine family went directly from an officer cadet to a commissioned officer."

Allan thought about this. It was certainly what he'd wanted. All he had to do was say yes, and he'd have his promotion.

But that's the old me.

Around and around in his mind, he couldn't let go of Lloyd's aspirations of being a cool soldier.

Which meant...

"............Heh." He grinned and went with what his heart said to do. "If I might offer a suggestion—"

Meanwhile, Choline was waiting for someone outside the school campus.

"—Yo, sorry to keep you."

She turned to find Chrome standing there, his square frame dressed in a military uniform.

"—Ha-ha, I knew that would look good on ya!" She gave him a few hearty slaps on the arm before a wistful look crossed her face. "—You doin' this for Merthophan?"

"Something like that. I feel like I could have stopped him, somehow."

"...And...where is he, exactly?"

"Heh, so you did have a thing for him."

"Wha—?!" Choline turned bright red.

"Heh-heh," Chrome chuckled. "Even I could tell... Although I bet ole stone-face never had a clue."

Choline's foot punted Chrome right in the butt.

"Gah!"

"Let me be clear, Chrome. We may both be teachers here, but I've got seniority. I tell ya to go buy a *yakisoba* sandwich for me, and I don't wanna hear a peep from you. And no coming back with a croquette sandwich just cause they're out!"

"Oww...ha-ha-ha, harsh." He rubbed his butt.

After she'd recovered her cool, Choline dragged the topic back to her question. "So, where is he? What's he up to?"

"Don't spread this around...but he's been sent to the frontier. Forced to labor in the deadliest conditions, I hear."

"Hard labor?"

"In a sense...but it's not his body that's being pushed to the breaking point." Chrome trailed off, staring into the distance—toward a certain village.

"—It's his values."

At said frontier, Merthophan was standing in a kitchen, washing dishes with a trace of desperation in the village of Kunlun.

The sweat on his brow wasn't from hard labor. It was more of a cold sweat.

A natural reaction. After all...

What's with this damn village?!

Gorging themselves in front of him were just a few of the villagers, each every bit as terrifyingly powerful as Lloyd himself.

"Merthophan's a decent cook, but I miss Lloyd's risotto, for sure."

"Yeah...but I hope he's doing all right. Our weak little chicklet..."

"Hey! No need to be rude!"

"Ma, you say that now, but you beat him in arm wrestling years ago!"

""""Ah-ha-ha-ha-ha-ha!""""

Merthophan was getting good at washing dishes even as his eyes popped out of his head.

They call Lloyd weak...

The village chief appeared behind him, her pigtails bouncing up and down.

"Merthophan! How 'bout ya clean up my second villa next?"

"...Certainly," he squeaked, his voice cracking and creaking in fear.

He couldn't get used to the horrifying power lurking within this girl. Merthophan followed after her, a good three paces behind, being careful not to step on her shadow.

"Well?" she asked. "Getting used to this place?"

"...*Never*," he replied, eyes practically popping out and rolling to the back of his head.

She laughed wryly. "Well, I hear tell the demon lord did a real number on you, accordin' to Marie... Figured this village would do wonders for any lingering guilt or gloom. Sweet kid, huh? I've always liked that about her."

"........." He grimaced (feat. bug-eyes).

"Anyway, after you've finished cleaning, we'll need help with the wheat fields. I'll have you know our people ain't good at managing the details, so if you can learn how to handle all that, it'll be a big help."

"Wheat?"

"Darn right. Wheat that you can harvest year round."

"Huh?"

Merthophan (feat. bug-eyes) clearly looked like he had no idea what she was talking about, so Alka pointed at the field in the distance.

The wheat was a lovely shade of gold, clearly ready to harvest.

Impossible...it was still green when I arrived!

(Side note: Wheat can be harvested anywhere from early summer to midautumn, depending on the climate. Definitely not all year long.)

The chief of this so-not-normal village filled him in.

"You see, the locust demon lord near about caused a famine on the entire continent a little while back. So I used a few runes to improve the plants. And once we'd distributed it everywhere, it seemed like a real pain to go back, you know, so we're still growing it. But that means we've got to harvest, like, every month, so managing the fields has been a real hassle!"

The grumbling in the latter half never reached his ears.

"…The wheat…that saved the continent…"

"Anyway, when villages are hit with natural disasters or droughts, we take this wheat to 'em. Look after it well!"

"Wait, you mean—?! During the famine! The one who brought everyone wheat was—?"

Alka held up a hand. "Don't ask. But…think of it this way: The locust demon lord might just revive someday, and we'll have less people turning out like you. Well, that sure motivates you to look after the wheat, doesn't it?"

She grinned at him. There were tears gushing down his cheeks.

"I…I will! I'll make sure it grows right!"

His stone face had crumbled completely.

Alka nodded, satisfied. "Anyway, I reckon we're gonna work you hard until those stiff face muscles and the inside of your head are nice and soft… Might be pretty rough for someone with as much common sense as you."

"—Very." Merthophan bowed his head low.

Alka waggled her fingers and turned toward her home. "Oh," she said. "Clean up that house there. I'm gonna go teleport back to Azami real quick."

"……gerk."

With tears freely streaming down his face, the word *teleport* made his eyes roll back again, as a trail of snot dripped from his face.

Alka vanished, leaving him laughing emptily as the snot dried in place.

"Ha-ha…teleporting…ha-ha-ha."

If this village banded together and started an invasion, the rest of the continent wouldn't last a month. That much was clear to him. Merthophan squinted, staring into the distance as he smiled.

"—Thank god for peace," he said. "Ha-ha-ha."

The spring breeze brought the smell of ripe wheat as it brushed across his cheeks and caused the field to ripple under the wind.

His tears were already dry.

*   *   *

Back in the general store, Marie was in her usual chair, sipping coffee, a relaxed smile on her face as morning sunlight streamed through the windows. She glanced at a clock, as if she was expecting someone—which was when Alka teleported into her closet.

Pushing through the clothing hanging inside with practiced ease, Alka straightened out her pigtails and made sure her outfit was in order.

"Oh, good morning, Master."

"Morning, Marie. How's the king doing?"

Alka checked herself in the mirror, then spun toward Marie with a smile as her pigtails flounced on her head.

"Much better. Thanks to you... His biggest injury is in the arm Lloyd batted aside, but it's on the mend."

Marie took an elegant sip of coffee. Alka pattered over and plopped down on a chair next to her as Marie slid a cup of coffee loaded with milk and sugar in her direction.

"I reckon you're not going back to the princess thing?"

"...Well, I sort of got used to living here," Marie admitted sheepishly. "Better than getting forced into some political marriage."

"I see...and..." Alka was starting to fidget.

Marie grinned and pointed to the back. "Hee-hee-hee... Lloyd should be changing into his uniform at the moment. The start of your adorable boy's adventure. Give him a moment to get ready."

But no sooner had the words left her mouth than Alka leaped to her feet, crystal in hand, making a beeline toward the room in back.

"Whoo-hoo! I can't wait any longer!"

"Wha—? Hey! He's still changing, *loli* Grandma!"

Alka pushed Marie away and flung open the door.

"........Eek! Wh-what are you doing here, Chief? I'm changing!"

Lloyd let out a very girlish shriek. His uniform was only half on.

"I reckon it's perfect timing!" Alka bellowed, spurting blood from her nose as she began using the crystal to record all sorts of compromising and illicit images without his consent.

"Master!" Marie yelled. "You can't record this! Lloyd, hurry up and get yourself decent!"

"Bweh-heh-heh… You're sure easy on the eyes! Nothing like a uniform half on! You know how long I've waited for this?! It was worth all the work I put into it!"

Alka's display of depravity made Marie's head light up with an idea. Oh lord. If only she was wrong.

With that dim hope in mind, she asked, "Master…is the reason you wanted Lloyd to enlist…?"

"Darn tootin'! The delectable contrast between his feminine features and that manly uniform! That's why I made him read all those military novels! …It's perfect! It's destroying me!" she spouted, covered in her own blood.

Marie shot the grandma a look of contempt. "You're the absolute worst," she spat.

But Alka's dumb military fetish had inadvertently saved the kingdom, so she couldn't be too mad.

Lloyd yanked his uniform on at last.

"Marie! Thank you so much! I'm finally a soldier…an officer cadet, at least!"

He looked so happy that all of Marie's gloom vanished into thin air, and she smiled back. "That's great," she agreed. "But who got you enlisted?"

The matter with Merthophan had been kept top secret. Before Marie had a chance to use her authority to argue on his behalf, he'd already received orders to join the academy. Thanks (?) to this strange event, she was able to avoid the thorny issues of keeping her promise to make Selen his roommate or the Sir-Lloyd-will-do-anything ticket, but Marie was left wondering.

As these thoughts ran through her mind, the shop door slammed open, and Selen and Riho came tumbling in.

"Oh, Sir Lloyd! I've been longing for the day when the two of us could walk to school together!"

"Yo, Lloyd! Lookin' good!"

Their arrival was met with a suspicious look from Alka, whose nose was still bleeding.

"Who are you…?" she asked.

Selen's look was equally wary. "Who are *you*…?"

Riho looked dubiously at the chief but also broke out in a cold sweat. "…Uh, yo, this kid's even more dangerous than Lloyd…"

Lloyd happily introduced everyone, missing the tension in the room.

"Um, this is the chief of my village, Alka. And these are my friends, Selen and Riho."

Riho looked slightly bashful to be introduced as a friend, but Selen's frown stayed put. As did Alka's.

"Friends?" Alka growled.

"For the moment," Selen purred.

Each had instantly identified the other as a rival, and their glares were equal to two boxers facing each other in the ring.

"Knock it off, Selen… This little girl's even worse than Lloyd. Seriously."

If Riho had been Selen's cornerman, she'd have thrown all the towels on hand.

Selen's eyes went hollow. "We'll love each other against all odds," she intoned.

Meanwhile, Alka was sneaking up behind her, plotting something nefarious.

"…I reckon it's best to deal with vermin before they cause any harm…if I use these runes, you'll get the runs for days and your anus will sting like the day after you've gorged yourself on spicy food. Being trapped in a toilet stall for three days and three nights will make even the love of the century fade…"

Marie caught just enough of this brutal threat to snap into action. "Master! You can't—"

But even as she tried to stop the *loli* grandma from ruining Lloyd's celebration…

Slap!

"What?!"

The cursed belt around Selen's waist reached out and smacked the back of the hand that Alka was using to write the runes. Slapped like a child trying to sneak a taste of dinner, the chief blew on her stinging hand.

"Oh? Chief? Were you trying to do something? I'm afraid your evil deeds are useless in the face of the red string of fate binding Sir Lloyd to me—the bloodstained belt!" Selen looked proud.

Alka gave the thing a once-over. "Th-that's the skin of the Divine Beast, Vritra!"

"Uh, Master? What's that?"

"A legendary artifact from Kunlun that protects the one who wears it from all forms of malice!"

"How does she have—?"

Alka rubbed her forehead, explaining.

"You see, I decided to make some homemade pasta for Lloyd ages ago and used the skin as an apron. And before I knew it, I'd gotten it mixed into the dough. I was all like, 'Since when is flour so hard?' and used Excalibur to slice it, then I boiled it and slapped some tomato sauce on it and sautéed the whole thing, and it wound up cursed, but I didn't wanna just throw it out, so I put some metal bits on it, called it a cursed belt, and sold it to some merchant for pennies...but how is it here?!"

"It's called karma, *loli* Grandma."

A new visitor stepped into the shop, another figure who was oblivious to tensions rising within.

"Pardon me!"

Standing there was Allan. The moment Lloyd saw him, he ran over, bowing low. Everyone else blinked at this deferential treatment.

"Allan! I can't thank you enough for this!"

This unusually polite greeting left everyone looking at one another in confusion.

Riho darted over to Allan, demanding to know why he was getting special treatment. Let's pretend her jealousy wasn't at all transparent.

"Yo, Allan...why are *you* here? Since when are you and Lloyd close?"

©Nao Watanuki

"What else, Mercenary? I'm the one who got Lloyd enlisted."

""""Hunh?!"""""

Everyone gawked at him.

"You see," Allan explained, "Lloyd saved my ass during that monster attack. I ended up running around trying to help, and the higher-ups wanted to reward those efforts. And I suggested they could repay me by allowing Lloyd to join us."

"...Where'd all your talk about promotion go?" Selen asked.

Allan looked sheepish. "W-well, I'm not in as big a rush anymore. And making Lloyd's hopes and dreams come true is the least I can do. As his student."

"Student?"

"Well, he hasn't actually accepted me yet. 'I've got nothing to teach anybody,' he says."

Selen stepped forward, surrounded by a pitch-black aura. "I see... so you're the root of evil? The one who ruined my plans to get Lloyd enlisted and force him to be my roommate as a reward? The one who swiped the rights to the Sir-Lloyd-will-do-anything ticket?"

"...What the hell are you talking about?"

Alka had been watching all this silently, but suddenly, her entire body started convulsing. "......Lloyd *is* cute enough," she muttered. "I reckon I should've been on guard against this threat from the get-go..."

"Um, Master?"

"All righty, time to level the country! I reckon all rotten oranges must be exterminated!"

"*Loli* Grandma! You can't treat entire countries like rotten oranges! Stop! ...Hey, people! Hold this pip-squeak down! She's gonna destroy the country!"

Allan refused to help the efforts to restrain the little girl with an exasperated expression. But his following words just made everything worse.

"Now, now, witch lady. I'm not laying my hands on any little girls! Mm? Wait, I've seen her..."

"You tellin' me that you're resisting the temptation of a girl…as cute as *me*?! This guy is the real deal!"

Marie blew her fuse, all the while wondering if Allan was deliberately winding her up. Her bellow echoed through the shop. "Arghhhh! Go home, *loli* Grandma! The rest of you, go to school!"

Hearing the shouts down the street, her neighbors on the East Side all thought: "Another busy day!" "Proof that all is peaceful."

"Oh, good morning! I'm off to school!"

No one realized the boy—Lloyd—spouting greetings as he passed, had protected all of them.

After all, that was the stuff of fiction: Suppose an ordinary boy from the neighborhood shop was secretly the hero who'd saved the country.

Afterword

I don't think it's ever too late to start something.

I was in my thirties. When I was trying to decide what to start, I remembered getting praise for my writing and recalled everyone laughing at a sketch that I'd written in the past. That's when I made up my mind to pick up my pen again.

I felt like I could bring some things to the table because I started at that age.

…And with that as my driving force, I wrote like a madman.

Everything I'd had stored up inside me.

Everything I'd thought was fun.

Everything that had got to me.

All the while believing that if I could get all that down, it would reach others.

And the first novel was called *Butt-Naked Berserker Shimamura.*

Let me say again: I don't think it's ever too late to start something.

But there are, well…there are times when I realize that it's too late to fix my mistakes. You know, as a human being. My entire existence. These results are proof.

Hello and good evening. My name is Toshio Satou.

I'd like to thank you for picking up *Suppose a Kid from the Last Dungeon Boonies Moved to a Starter Town.*

First, the formalities.

To my illustrator, Nao Watanuki: Thank you for all the lovely illustrations. I'll never forget how it felt to see Lloyd for the first time.

To Maizou, who agreed to be my editor: Thank you for offering guidance when I was just trying to do something but didn't know right from left.

My head will be forever bowed to everyone in the GA Bunko editorial department, the team in sales and marketing, and the proofreaders.

Thank you to my fellow 8th Award recipients for the encouragement that you've offered via messages on Line.

And to my parents: You were the first I told the good news about the award, and I'll never forget how you said, "Yeah, yeah, could you buy us some Buff-rin?" That really cooled my head off, for sure.

Finally, I'd like to thank my readers once again.

I hope we meet again in Volume 2.

TOSHIO SATOU

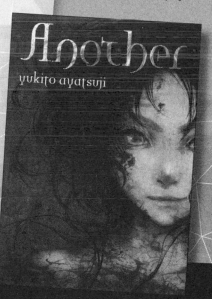